P9-BYU-731

it's all
about us

it's all
about us

a novel

SHELLEY ADINA

NEW YORK
BOSTON
NASHVILLE

Scriptures noted NIV are taken from the HOLY BIBLE: NEW INTERNATIONAL VERSION®. Copyright © 1973, 1978, 1984 by International Bible Society. Used by permission of Zondervan Publishing House. All rights reserved.

FaithWords
Hachette Book Group USA
237 Park Avenue
New York, NY 10017

Visit our Web site at www.faithwords.com.

FaithWords is a division of Hachette Book Group USA, Inc.
The FaithWords name and logo are trademarks of Hachette Book Group USA, Inc.

Printed in the United States of America

First Edition: May 2008
10 9 8 7 6 5 4 3 2 1

Library of Congress Cataloging-in-Publication Data

Adina, Shelley.
    It's all about us / Shelley Adina. — 1st ed.
        p. cm.
    ISBN-13: 978-0-446-17798-6
    ISBN-10: 0-446-17798-9
    1. Teenage girls—Fiction.   2. Schoolgirls—Fiction.   I. Title.
PS3602.A875I87   2008
813'.6—dc22   2007033272

For Jennifer Jackson

acknowledgments

This book wouldn't exist without the help of a number of people:

Jennifer Jackson, my agent, who told me, "If you write this, I can sell it." And she did.

Anne Horch, who became the head cheerleader of my team as soon as she saw the manuscript.

My first readers, Sarah, Julia, and Allie, who helped me keep it real, and my niece, Kailey, who provided a beautiful model for my heroine.

Patrick and Joanne, for the use of the mulch pile.

The original Grrls, who were in on this from the beginning and helped brainstorm titles and plots: Kristin Billerbeck, Marilyn Hilton, Dineen Miller, Camy Tang, and M. L. Tyndall.

The members of the Looney Bin, who can unravel anything from a plot knot to a revision letter: Diana Duncan, Tina Ferraro, Susan Gable, Cindy Procter-King, Catherine Mulvany, Anita Staley, and Debrah Williamson.

And, as always, Jeff, who has learned that research (a.k.a., watching high school movies or reading *Teen Vogue*) is tax deductible and therefore should not be interrupted.

it's all
about us

"And this is my prayer: that your love may abound more and more in knowledge and depth of insight, so that you may be able to discern what is best and may be pure and blameless until the day of Christ."
—*Philippians 1:9–10 (NIV)*

chapter 1

SOME THINGS YOU just know without being told. Like, you passed the math final (or you didn't). Your boyfriend isn't into you anymore and wants to break up. Vanessa Talbot has decided that since you're the New Girl, you have a big bull's-eye on your forehead and your junior year is going to be just as miserable as she can make it.

Carly once told me she used to wish she were me. Ha! That first week at Spencer Academy, I wouldn't have wished my life on anyone.

My name is Lissa Evelyn Mansfield, and since everything seemed to happen to me this quarter, we decided I'd be the one to write it all down. Maybe you'll think I'm some kind of drama queen, but I swear this is the truth. Don't listen to Gillian and Carly—they weren't there for some of it, so probably when they read this, it'll be news to them, too.

But I'm getting ahead of myself. When it all started, I didn't even know them. All I knew was that I was starting my junior year at the Spencer Academy of San Francisco, this private boarding school for trust fund kids and the offspring of the hopelessly rich, and I totally did not want to be there.

I mean, picture it: You go from having fun and being popular in tenth grade at Pacific High in Santa Barbara, where you can hang out on State Street or join a drumming circle or surf whenever you feel like it with all your friends, to being absolutely nobody in this massive old mansion where rich kids go because their parents don't have time to take care of them.

Not that my parents are like that. My dad's a movie director, and he's home whenever his shooting schedule allows it. When he's not, sometimes he flies us out to cool places like Barbados or Hungary for a week so we can be on location together. You've probably heard of my dad. He directed that big pirate movie that Warner Brothers did a couple of years ago. That's how he got on the radar of some of the big A-list directors, so when George (hey, he asked me to call him that, so it's not like I'm dropping names) rang him up from Marin and suggested they do a movie together, of course he said yes. I can't imagine anybody saying no to George, but anyway, that's why we're in San Francisco for the next two years. Since Dad's going to be out at the Ranch or on location so much, and my sister, Jolie, is at UCLA (film school, what else—she's a daddy's girl and she admits it), and my mom's dividing her time among all of us, I had the choice of going to boarding school or having a live-in. Boarding school sounded fun in a Harry Potter kind of way, so I picked that.

Sigh. That was before I realized how lonely it is being the New Girl. Before the full effect of my breakup really hit. Before I knew about Vanessa Talbot, who I swear would make the perfect girlfriend for a warlock.

And speaking of witch . . .

"Melissa!"

Note: my name is *not* Melissa. But on the first day of classes, I'd made the mistake of correcting Vanessa, which meant that every time she saw me after that, she made a point of saying it wrong. The annoying part is that now people really think that's my name.

Vanessa, Emily Overton, and Dani Lavigne ("Yes, *that* Lavigne. Did I tell you she's my cousin?") are like this triad of terror at Spencer. Their parents are all fabulously wealthy—richer than my mom's family, even—and they never let you forget it. Vanessa and Dani have the genes to go with all that money, which means they look good in everything from designer dresses to street chic.

Vanessa's dark brown hair is cut so perfectly, it always falls into place when she moves. She has the kind of skin and dark eyes that might be from some Italian beauty somewhere in her family tree. Which, of course, means the camera loves her. It didn't take me long to figure out that there was likely to be a photographer or two somewhere on the grounds pretty much all the time, and nine times out of ten, Vanessa was the one they bagged. Her mom is minor royalty and the ex-wife of some U.N. Secretary or other, which means every time he gives a speech, a photographer shows up here. Believe me, seeing Vanessa in the halls at school and never knowing when she's going to pop out at me from the pages of *Teen People* or some society news Web site is just annoying. Can you say *overexposed?*

Anyway. Where was I? Dani has butterscotch-colored hair that she has highlighted at Biondi once a month, and big blue eyes that make her look way more innocent than she is. Emily is shorter and chunkier and could maybe be nice if you got her on her own, but she's not the kind that functions well outside of a clique.

Some people are born independent and some aren't. You should see Emily these days. All that money doesn't help her one bit out at the farm, where—

Okay, Gillian just told me I have to stop doing that. She says it's messing her up, like I'm telling her the ending when I'm supposed to be telling the beginning.

Not that it's all about her, okay? It's about us: me, Gillian, Carly,

Shani, Mac . . . and God. But just to make Gillian happy, I'll skip to the part where I met her, and she (and you) can see what I really thought of her. Ha. Maybe that'll make her stop reading over my shoulder.

So as I was saying, there they were—Vanessa, Emily, and Dani—standing between me and the dining room doors. "What's up?" I said, walking up to them when I should have turned and settled for something out of the snack machine at the other end of the hall.

"She doesn't know." Emily poked Dani. "Maybe we shouldn't tell her."

I did a fast mental check. Plaid skirt—okay. Oxfords—no embarrassing toilet paper. White blouse—buttoned, no stains. Slate blue cardigan—clean. Hair—freshly brushed.

They couldn't be talking about me personally, in which case I didn't need to hear it. "Whatever." I pushed past them and took two steps down the hall.

"Don't you want to hear about your new roommate?" Vanessa asked.

Roommate? At that point I'd survived for five days, and the only good things about them were the *crème brulée* in the dining room and the blessed privacy of my own room. What fresh disaster was this?

Oops. I'd stopped in my tracks and tipped them off that (a) I didn't know, and (b) I wanted to know. And when Vanessa knows you want something, she'll do everything she can not to let you have it.

"I think we should tell her," Emily said. "It would be kinder to get it over with."

"I'm sure I'll find out eventually." There, that sounded bored enough. "Byeee."

"I hope you like Chinese!" Dani whooped at her own cleverness, and the three of them floated off down the hall.

So I thought, *Great, maybe they're having* dim sum *today for lunch,* though what that had to do with my new roommate I had no idea. At that point it hadn't really sunk in that conversation with those three is a dangerous thing.

That had been my first mistake the previous Wednesday, when classes had officially begun. Conversation, I mean. You know, normal civilized discourse with someone you think might be a friend. Like a total dummy, I'd actually thought this about Vanessa, who'd pulled newbie duty, walking me down the hall to show me where my first class was. It turned out to not be my first class, but the teacher was nice about steering me to the right room, where I was, of course, late.

That should've been my first clue.

My second clue was when Vanessa invited me to eat with them and Dani managed to spill her Coke all over my uniform skirt, which is, as I said, plaid and made of this easy-clean fake wool that people with sensitive skin can wear. She'd jumped up, all full of apologies, and handed me napkins and stuff, but the fact remained that I had to go upstairs and change and then figure out how the laundry service worked, which meant I was late for Biology, too.

On Thursday Dani apologized again, and Vanessa loaned me some of her Bumble and bumble shampoo ("You can't use Paul Mitchell on gorgeous hair like yours—people get that stuff at the *drugstore* now"), and I was dumb enough to think that maybe things were looking up. Because really, the shampoo was superb. My hair is blond and I wear it long, but before you go hating me for it, it's fine and thick, and the fog we have here in San Francisco makes it go all frizzy. And it's foggy a lot. So this shampoo made it just coo with pleasure.

You're probably asking yourself why I bothered trying to be friends with these girls. The harrowing truth was, I was used to being in the A-list group. It never occurred to me that I wouldn't fit in with the popular girls at Spencer, once I figured out who they were.

Lucky me—Vanessa made that so easy. And I was so lonely and out of my depth that even she was looking good. Her dad had once backed one of my dad's films, so there was that minimal connection.

Too bad it wasn't enough.

jolie.mansfield	L, don't let them bug you. Some people are threatened by anything new. It's a compliment really.
LMansfield	You always find the bright side. Gahh. Love you, but not helping.
jolie.mansfield	What can I do?
LMansfield	I'd give absolutely anything to be back in S.B.
jolie.mansfield	:(
LMansfield	I want to hang with the kids from my youth group. Not worry about anything but the SPF of my sun block.
jolie.mansfield	It'll get better. Promise. Heard from Mom?
LMansfield	No. She's doing some fundraiser with Angelina. She's pretty busy.
jolie.mansfield	If you say so. Love you.

chapter 2

ISS MANSFIELD, may I have a moment?"

I'd put my phone away and was reaching for the very last *crème brulée*, but when I turned to see what Ms. Curzon wanted, the guy in line behind me snaked it. I fought back the urge to crack his hand against the stainless steel tray track and snatch the dessert from his broken fingers, and took a raspberry moussey-looking thing instead.

Needless to say, I wasn't feeling very Christian when I finally faced Ms. Curzon.

The principal (or headmistress, if you said it the way Ms. Curzon said it, with a cool British accent) was one of those women you expect to see in a collared T-shirt and pleated skirt, running across the lawn with a field-hockey stick following a healthy breakfast of bangers and mash. She was tall and thin and her hair looked like it had been whacked off by, well, herself, in front of the bathroom mirror. Like she couldn't care less what people thought of her looks. Maybe she just cared more what they thought of her school.

But when we'd come here to get me enrolled last week, my

mom went as breathless and fluttery as that time she sat next to Harrison Ford at a movie premiere.

"Natalie Curzon spent ten years in the Amazon jungle fighting for a nature conservancy," she whispered to me while the headmistress went into the outer office to get something. "Miramax wanted to film her story and had Hilary Swank attached to star, but she turned them down. Wouldn't give them the rights to her book, even though she could have retired on the money."

I figure ten years in an Amazon jungle is about as qualified as you can get to run a private school for rich people's kids.

I followed Ms. Curzon to a table at the back, where there seemed to be a one-woman show going on, starring a girl with hair so black it had blue highlights. In a New York accent that gave her a worldly-wise authority, she was telling the rest of the kids at the table some story that involved the Staten Island ferry and an accident. She had a song playing on her portable CD player like it was the score to the drama.

"Gillian, I'd like you to meet your new roommate," Ms. Curzon said.

Nobody paid any attention. Ms. Curzon said it again, louder.

Nada. Then, moving as swiftly as a jungle cat, Ms. Curzon whipped the player off the table, shut it up, and waited. In the sudden cone of silence, Gillian blinked at her, totally surprised.

"What?" she said.

"Gillian, this is your new roommate," Ms. Curzon told her, as if she hadn't repeated herself once already. "Lissa Mansfield, this is Gillian Chang."

Suddenly I realized what Dani had meant, the prejudiced little . . . darling.

The only dim someone in this room was me.

I nodded at Gillian Chang and gave her my best smile, but she only stared at me. "And this couldn't have waited 'til I was done?" Then she seemed to figure out who she was talking to. She glanced at the principal. "Sorry. Ma'am."

"Why don't I leave you two to get acquainted?" Ms. Curzon smiled at us, handed Gillian her player, and pushed off through the tables to go do whatever headmistresses did when they were minding their own business.

"Feel free to join us," Gillian said in a breezy tone that made it clear it was all the same to her whether I did or not.

You'd never guess we were destined to become best friends, would you? Gillian says she was only trying to be cool and not scream at me because I'm tall and blond and—her words, not mine—looked like I had the world in my pocket to play with.

Right, like I'd scream at her because she's brilliant and plays about a dozen different musical instruments and can say the periodic table of the elements backwards.

Carly says we should be grateful God gave us all different gifts. Which is her nice way of saying, Just shut up and get on with the story.

So I sat across from my new roomie, and then I saw what was on her tray.

Crème brulée.

I swear, at that moment if I wasn't sure that God loved me, I'd think He was trying to build my character or something.

Gillian launched back into her story and I got the gist of it. She'd actually been on the ferry when it missed its berth, crashed, and sank right there in the harbor. Stuff like that never happens to me.

"Did you have to go to the hospital?" a kid who looked to be a sophomore asked.

"No, I got squashed between these two old ladies, and we all kind of fell against the fender of a car. The lady on the bottom got the worst of it. Hey, want to hear what happened when we got stuck in the elevator inside the Eiffel Tower? I have some cool Django Reinhardt here to get us in the mood."

There went the CD player again. I lost interest. Jangle who? Tribulations might be sent to test the soul, but did that mean you had to sit with them for your whole lunch hour?

What I needed here was to just concentrate on ingesting food. I needed to keep my strength up for Math, not because we were starting trig, but because Callum McCloud sat one row over from me and two seats up, and I wanted all five senses in working order.

Not that I'd use my sense of taste on him. Okay, yes, I would. Like, if he ever kissed me. But for now, hearing and seeing would have to do, and maybe even touching and smelling if I got lucky during the rush for the door at the end of class.

Callum McCloud was the hottest thing I'd seen since I'd arrived. By Thursday I'd developed this weird heat-seeking radar where he was concerned. I could pick his blond head out of a crowd anywhere, which wasn't that hard because he was tall and the entire privileged student body numbered maybe two hundred, including day students like him. Sometimes I just had to turn to see him going into a classroom or crossing the quad, the lawn in the center of the square formed by the building's wings.

He had a lean, tan body, eyes that looked like they could see through your soul, and, from what I'd seen, he seemed to be nice, too. He did his share of joking around, but they weren't mean jokes. I'd even seen him pick up a spilled lapful of books for Carrie Whiteside, who rolled around on an electric scooter because there was something wrong with her legs.

In short, I was crushing bad on Callum, and I wanted him to be crushing just as bad on me.

Only two things stood in my way:

1. The fact that he didn't know I was alive.
2. Vanessa Talbot.

BLoyola   Who's the new girl?

VTalbot   Don't ask.

BLoyola   On your bad side already, V? She's cute.

VTalbot   If you like 'em blond and dumb. Which I think you do.

BLoyola   Meow. Single?

VTalbot   Who, me?

BLoyola   Haha.

VTalbot   Why don't you ask her? I'm not your social director.

————

BLoyola   Catfight!

CMcCloud   ??

BLoyola   The lovely Talbot has a hate on for the new girl.

CMcCloud   ??

BLoyola   You blind? The blonde behind you in Trig. Yowza. Smokin'.

CMcCloud   You interested?

BLoyola   Maybe. You?

CMcCloud   If I was, I wouldn't tell you. May as well put out a press release.

BLoyola   Paranoid much?

chapter 3

I HOPE THERE'S NO practical application for trigonometry out there in the real world, because with Callum practically within touching distance, I was totally blanking on it. But even though I tried to oh-so-casually reach the door when he did, Vanessa got there before me and dragged him off to their next class together.

I will prevail, I thought. *Just give me time.*

The nice thing was, the buzz of having locked eyes with him as he turned to put something in his backpack lasted through the rest of Monday afternoon (Psychology and Spanish)—right up until the moment I walked through the door of my room and was reminded that You Are Not Alone.

The loud Asian girl from New York stood on the second bed, which was covered in boxes and two huge Louis Vuitton suitcases, trying to get a paper parasol with cranes painted on it into the corner above the wall unit, where she must have just put a lamp with a red bulb.

I took my earphones out. "What are you doing?"

"What does it look like? Help me with this, would you?"

I took in the situation. "The parasol's top-heavy. That's why it keeps rolling off. You need to move the lamp back so the handle can go down the back of the wall unit."

Mission accomplished. Immediately, that corner of the room was bathed in this rosy glow, the kind that reminds you of pajama parties and playing Truth or Dare. Frankly, Gillian Chang didn't look like a pajama-party kind of girl. Or the kind you shared your deepest, darkest truths with.

Which shows you how little I knew about her then.

She jumped off the bed and pulled a big silk shawl out of one of the suitcases. And I mean really big. It would have covered the dining room table in our house in Santa Barbara, which seated eighteen.

Now, wait just a minute. "Are you going to put that up, too? You know, you might ask me whether I want my room to look like Inara's boudoir before you start hanging stuff all over it."

Gillian turned and stared at me like I was speaking Mandarin. "What?"

"You know. Inara, from *Firefly*. You're going to make the room look like her shuttle, all hung with silk and brocade. Which is fine for a Companion, but it's not my style."

"Oh, it's not." Azure blue silk with little gold figures of birds all over it bunched between her hands. "Well, maybe it's mine. And if I have to live here, I'm going to make it look like home."

"Keep it on your half of the room, then."

The thing you have to understand about Spencer is that it used to be some countess's house back in the early nineteen hundreds. When the earl died in England, he left her pots of money, so she came to California and built this place with the intent that it would be a school for the nobs' kids and she'd live in part of it. Consequently the rooms are not your standard dorm rooms. They're huge, with ten-foot ceilings and wainscoting, and some of them even have chandeliers. So hanging a massive piece of royal-blue silk on the wall makes quite a fashion statement . . . one I wasn't prepared to live with.

"You have to begin as you mean to go on," my great-grandma told me once when I was little, like in first grade. I hadn't begun well with Vanessa, so I was going to make up for that, starting now.

Gillian's bed was on one side, with her desk and wall unit, and mine was on the other, with a big window in between. The only place you could hang something like her silk tablecloth was on the wall next to the door, where I already had hung my bulletin board and a couple of my favorite posters. And I wasn't taking them down.

I'd begin the way I meant to go on. After all, what else might be in the depths of those suitcases? What if she practiced an Eastern religion? What if she had a statue of the Buddha in there? It would be none of my business if this was her own room, but I wasn't too keen about sharing space with graven idols, of choking on the smell of incense, of maybe even hearing her chant mantras or whatever it was practitioners of Eastern religions did.

Uh-uh. Ain't gonna happen.

"There isn't room," she said. "It should go there, by the door."

"Sorry," I said, and put my earphones back in.

So what did she do? She marched over and pulled the tacks out of my *Don Juan DeMarco* movie poster, which is the hottest Johnny Depp movie of all time. She rolled it up (neatly, Gillian reminds me) and put it on one of my shelves, then went to work on the *Edward Scissorhands* one.

"Hey!"

"We're sharing this room. And sharing, in case you didn't learn this when you were potty-trained, means we each get equal space."

"We do have equal space. Yours is on that side. Mine is on this side. And those posters were on my side."

"Please tell me you're not going to make me draw a line down the middle of this room. Even you can't be that selfish."

Even me? She'd known me for, what, a grand total of five minutes?

"You beey—" I caught myself just in time. I'd come to Christ three years before, but there are some verbal habits that take a long time to change, especially in moments of stress. My dad swears like a pirate, so I come by it honestly. And I'm trying to overcome it, equally as honestly.

"What did you almost call me?" Gillian's eyes narrowed with dislike. With my luck, she probably had a black belt and I was about to become a pile of crumpled limbs on the floor.

"Nothing."

"I heard you. You almost called me a b—"

"But I didn't, did I?"

"You wanted to. And intent is just as bad as action."

Oh, brother. What was she in, eleventh-grade pre-law? "Give it a rest, Gillian. And put those posters back."

"Put them back yourself. After I get my hanging up."

"Fine." I flopped on the bed and pulled out my Psych homework. "They'll go over it. I'll try not to damage it with too many tack holes."

Outmaneuvered you on that one, didn't I, sweetie?

I barely had time to start feeling smug when she got into my face. "You snotty, stuck-up little *mo guai nuer!* You touch my hanging and you'll be sorry."

Okay, it's one thing to swear in English, but no way was I letting anyone swear at me in Mandarin. Who knew what she was calling me?

"I am not stuck-up."

"Oh, yeah? You could have fooled me. You parade around here with your nose in the air like you're the Queen of England and the rest of us are peasants. You order me around and threaten to damage my stuff. In the real world, that is stuck-up."

"Right, like you live in the real world." All that about the ferry and the Eiffel Tower was probably made up. Kids did it all the time—they came to a new school and invented a life just because they were scared and wanted people to think they were cool.

"At least I'm not a spoiled rich kid who treats people like trash and needs a good spanking."

I'd had just about enough of Miss Loudmouth here. I was not spoiled, and I treated people the way I wanted to be treated, just like Jesus said.

Present company excepted.

"Oh, yeah? I'd like to see you try."

Gillian glared daggers at me. "I'm going to do even better than that." She paused, and a light came into her eyes, as if she'd thought of the most evil punishment ever devised. "I'm going to pray for you."

chapter 4

I STARED AT HER.

Then I recovered and closed my mouth, which had been hanging open in astonishment. She couldn't have meant what I thought she meant.

"Praying to your friend the Buddha won't get you a thing where I'm concerned," I informed her. "And you can forget about putting him anywhere I can see him."

"My—" She blinked at me. "For heaven's sake, pull the stereotype out of your eye, would you? My prayers go to Jesus."

It takes a lot to render me completely speechless, but this did it.

Gillian was a Christian. We both were—sisters under grace—and what were we doing? Screaming at each other like a pair of banshees who had never heard the name of Jesus in our whole lives.

I felt my eyes fill with tears, and I sat with a thump on the bed, my hand over my guilty, uncontrollable, hateful mouth. When was I ever going to learn to shut up?

Because she was completely right. I had superimposed a big old ugly stereotype right over her, and said all those nasty things to it instead of taking the time to get to know the real girl underneath. I had seen my dumb assumptions instead of an actual person. She had every right to be angry with me.

So she wanted to hang some blue silk on the wall. Big deal. I had turned it into a whole religion and condemned her for it, all in my imagination. No wonder she thought I didn't live in the real world. I'd just proven it, hadn't I?

"I'm so sorry," I managed to say without breaking down and crying in front of her, though I was close. Luckily I had a Kleenex in my tote. I dug it out and blew my nose.

She looked a little surprised, but I didn't know if it was because of the snotty Kleenex or because I'd apologized.

"I meant it." Her tone was aggressive, as if I was going to resume the attack and she was getting ready for me. "I'm going to pray for you."

"I wish you would," I said with a sigh. That took her back a bit. She must not have expected me to agree with her. "My mouth gets me into trouble a dozen times a day. I pray and pray about it, but it doesn't seem to help. Do you think God has call-waiting and He's just busy with everyone else but me?"

This time it was Gillian's mouth that hung open. "Are you saying—"

I nodded. "Pretty lousy example of loving my sister, huh?" I knew I was giving her a giant opening for another attack.

Humiliation, thy name is Lissa.

"I'm sorry I said that about the Buddha," I went on. "I'm just having a really bad week."

She tossed the silk over the Celtic harp standing in the corner— how had I missed that?—where it draped in a glorious spill of color, and sat on the ergonomically correct chair in front of my desk.

"You're not the only one. I'm sorry I called you all those names."

I'd had most of them thrown at me before, but they'd never hurt quite like this. "What does that mean, what you said? *Mo guai* whatever."

Her neck and forehead flushed red. "*Mo guai nuer.* It means 'evil girl.' The closest you can come in Mandarin to—uh, you know."

"Ouch. Well, it was accurate, for what that's worth."

"I still shouldn't have said it."

I looked at her, hoping that this moment of honesty would last for a few more seconds before we set each other off again. "Do I really come off as snotty and stuck-up? Because that's the last thing I want."

She rubbed at a speck of something on the desk. "Maybe. A little."

Oh, great. No wonder Vanessa thought I was a threat. "I don't see how. I'm just trying to figure things out around here. Get through a day without Vanessa and her crew dumping on me. How does that translate to being stuck-up?"

"Gimme a break, Mansfield. You're tall and blond and you have cheekbones. That's enough reason for anybody to dump on you."

"Unlike you. You had a whole audience hanging on your every word."

"Not the A-group."

"Maybe not, but at least you're making friends. Not one person except Vanessa, Emily, and Dani has talked to me since I started, and those three only do it so they can set me up for something."

"You just answered your own question. If you're hanging around with them, of course no one's going to talk to you. Please tell me you're not really that clueless."

I shot her an annoyed glance. "Are you always this brutal?"

"I call 'em like I see 'em, you know? And it doesn't take a genius to figure out that the A-group only talks to other people in the A-group. Normal people aren't going to stick their necks out and risk getting their heads bitten off."

"Except me."

"So why do you keep going back for more?"

Why did I? Gillian made me feel like a dope—a blond dope who couldn't tell that someone was abusing her and kept going back in hopes that eventually she'd pay her dues and be accepted.

Can you say *masochist*?

"I used to be popular. At my old school." How feeble was that?

"Were you popular, or did people actually like you?"

"There's a difference?"

"Of course there's a difference." Gillian scooted the chair forward a little and I prepared for another whack on the old self-confidence. "I mean, what do you want? For a bunch of backstabbing fashionistas to invite you through the sacred portal to hang out with them? Or do you want friends who actually might think you have a brain and something to share? Who like you just because you get up in the morning, not because there's something in it for them?"

Okay, this was getting just the slightest bit annoying. "You sound like my sister."

"In case you forgot, I *am* your sister."

She had a point. And what she said might even be right. But—

"It can't go on much longer," I said. "It's like an initiation, and when it's over, they're your friends. And besides—"

"Besides what?"

"There's this guy."

Gillian exhaled, as though I'd just taken away her last hope. Then she smiled. Humoring me. "I bet."

"No, really. You've probably seen him." When I pictured Callum McCloud, putting up with Vanessa and Dani didn't seem so bad. "He is so hot he makes the air sizzle around him. And he hangs around with those girls. He and Brett Loyola and Todd Runyon."

"I've heard about Todd Runyon." She made him sound like an ax murderer. "And I haven't even been here twenty-four hours."

"I don't care about Todd." I waved a hand, as if to push the idea of him away. "We were talking about Callum McCloud."

"Oh."

"Oh, what?"

"Nothing. I just heard he and Vanessa were together, that's all. But, you know, unrequited love is kind of romantic."

Whack. "They're not together. If they were, believe me, Vanessa would be taking out ads in the *Chronicle* and putting up banners in the hallways."

"Maybe he likes her. Unofficially."

"Could you look on the bright side? All I have to do is hang around with them and he'll see I'm totally the one he wants. Because, believe me, I'd be better for him than Vanessa by, like, a factor of a hundred."

I hadn't had trouble getting boys' attention since I'd graduated out of my training bra. And I had every intention of making Callum not only see me, but ask me out, too. And after that, it wouldn't matter what Vanessa or Dani or anybody thought. Especially a certain person at Pacific High who dumped me flat on my face exactly one week before we moved up here. Someone who swore I was his one and only, and with whom I'd made plans for Christmas that involved him flying up to be my date at whatever Spencer's equivalent of a holiday party was.

Needless to say, those plans had crashed and burned and now lay in cinders all around me.

I'd get the hottest guy in school, I swore to myself. And when I had him, I'd be popular by default. Despite Vanessa Talbot. Despite my bruised self-confidence. And no matter what my opinionated roommate thought.

After all, just because she was a Christian didn't mean she was right about everything.

✉

To: lmansfield@spenceracad.edu
From: jolie.mansfield@film.ucla.edu
Date: September 22, 2008
Re: First week

Hey girl,

Thanx for sending me your addy. Time for a real message instead of
IMs. It's been crazy around here but I'm loving it. Found out our term
project is a nonfic documentary about a person or organization. I
figure this is a perfect opportunity to do a thing on Pastor Norman
and his soup kitchen on the beach. What do you think?

But enough about me. I know you're having a tough time. I'm sorry,
kiddo. It was rough leaving PHS but I kinda envy you being up there
in Fog City. I bet there's some great opportunities to talk about God
to people. You can bet I'm gonna let my documentary do the talking
for me :) Maybe Dad will even watch it.

And as far as that loser Aidan, I think you're well rid of him. Nobody
sets my sister up and dumps her for the homecoming queen without
consequences. Good grief, what a cliché he is. You deserve better. This
Callum guy sounds nice, but don't let looks be all that. He's got to have
more to be someone you can care about, right? Is he a Christian?

Oops, gotta go. Study group starts in ten and I have to hustle all the
way across campus.

Love you a million times—

Jolie

....

✉

To: lmansfield@spenceracad.edu
From: kazg@hotmail.com
Date: September 22, 2008
Re: How ya doin'?

Hey. I keep hoping I'm gonna wake up and find out that your transfer
up north was a bad dream. So far the nightmare continues.

Got some good classes. Honors English and Spanish. We could have
done that together, huh? And Horton for Bio. At least he won't kick
me out for asking questions—but first roll he called me "Charles." Like
anyone has done that since first grade. Didn't take long to educate
him :)

What about you? You probably have 17 boyfriends by now. Haha.
Check in when you can.

Kaz

....

chapter 5

THE NEXT MORNING, as I was putting my contacts in, Gillian pointed her toothbrush at me. Fortunately, she hadn't started using it yet.

"We should start a prayer circle."

I blinked and my lens slid into place. This meant that I could see half of her clearly. "Okay. But don't you mean a prayer *pair*? It's kinda hard to form a circle with just the two of us."

"No, no. That's the point. We need to invite people. There must be more Christians at Spencer than just you and me."

I blinked the second lens in and glanced at her as I screwed the top on its little container that looked like a fat lipstick. "I wouldn't count on it."

She spat out a mouthful of toothpaste and rinsed her mouth. "Why?"

"You've only been here for a day. I've been here since last week, and I haven't seen a single sign of it. No posters, no notices, no praise music coming from behind a door, nothing."

"That doesn't mean anything. We can do stuff like that. I can make a notice on my laptop in about ten seconds. And I must have a gig of praise music on my iPod. Maybe two, if you include videos."

"And you think that'll make the Christians come sneaking out of the undergrowth?"

She looked at me a little oddly. "Why would they need to sneak?" She held up her uniform skirt on its hanger. "Do we really have to wear this every single day?"

"Yes. And outside of classes, no tops showing the midriff, no thongs, and your skirts have to meet the finger test."

"How would they know if I was wearing a thong? The rest I get."

I ignored her. "Also, no T-shirts with slogans or pictures."

"Now, that is just wrong."

"You can wear them off-campus, just not at school."

"Why, for Pete's sake?"

I shrugged. "It violates our First Amendment rights, if you ask me."

Her eyes lit up. "We should protest! This is California, after all. I've never protested before. It could be fun."

I finished dressing and checked myself out in the full-length mirror on the inside of the wardrobe door. "You're going to be busy, between class and advertising a prayer circle and protesting. When are you going to do your homework?"

Shrugging on her cardigan, she gave me another look. "What's this 'you' stuff? Aren't you in on it with me?"

I sighed and closed the wardrobe door. "Gillian, it's not my style to go around advertising my faith. If someone approaches me to ask about it, that's one thing, but I'm not putting my name on a poster and deliberately inviting—" I stopped.

"Inviting who?"

I hesitated. "People."

"That's not what you were about to say. Come on. Spill."

"Inviting more grief. I already feel like a moving target. If I put up posters for a prayer circle, it'll just give Vanessa and Emily and Dani more ammunition."

"So? Why do you care what they think?"

She wasn't getting it. "I already told you last night. I want them to be my friends."

"Well, I don't." Gillian grabbed a backpack that looked as though it had been through a war. Maybe it had—it was army surplus, by the look of it, and covered in patches from places like Egypt and Hong Kong. I, on the other hand, used a Kate Spade tote instead of a backpack. It was so pretty, I was sure I'd cry when I got the first scuff mark on it.

You're probably thinking, *Oh, quit whining and get something practical that you don't care about,* but that's not the way I'm made. I like nice things. There's no sin in that, and my mom can afford it.

"I think you're hiding your light under a bushel." We clattered down the grand staircase, heading for the dining room and breakfast. "And you know what Jesus said about that."

"Jesus never went to school with Vanessa Talbot," I pointed out, a little acidly.

"Yeah, but think about it. He didn't just talk to people about a prayer circle. He told them He was the Son of God. That's, like, orders of magnitude harder. But He still did it."

You'll notice that it's nearly impossible to win an argument with Gillian. She has no fear of pulling out the big guns and blasting you until you beg for mercy.

"Nobody is stopping you from doing whatever you want," I said as we walked into the dining room. "I'm happy to be in the prayer circle. But I'm not going to go around collaring people and asking them if they want to join."

"But that's not what I—"

"Oh, look, oatmeal for breakfast. Again."

Gillian isn't dumb. She'll let you change the subject. But you can bet she'll circle back around to it later, like a shark. Just when you thought it was safe.

She just told me to tell you that's called *persistence,* but I think it's more than that. Part of it has to do with the fact that she's totally in love with Jesus and she'll do whatever it takes so that you feel the same way. I love this about her, but right then, I couldn't see it. All I saw was the look of evil delight on Vanessa Talbot's face as she latched onto yet one more reason to laugh at me.

After breakfast, Gillian and I went our separate ways, she to her core class and me to my free period. You'd think the administration would schedule these at the end of the day, but no. Mine started at eight forty-five, twice a week. At least I could have a second cup of coffee if I wanted to, or take a tray up to our room, but as it turned out, I passed the library on the ground floor and spotted Callum McCloud all by his yummy self at a table by the window.

I took about three seconds to wonder (a) what it was about this guy that made my breathing speed up and the nape of my neck tingle, and (b) whether I actually had the guts to walk in and sit down across from him.

I didn't have an answer to (a), but by the fourth second, I sure had one for (b).

He looked up from whatever he was writing in his notebook as I dropped my tote on the floor and slid into the empty chair.

"Hey."

His voice was perfect. Not too much bass, and no tenor. (Tenors are fine for Italian opera, but not on hot guys with green eyes and lashes to die for.)

"Hi," I said. "Okay if I sit here?"

He shrugged, but the half smile made it an invitation. "If you want."

Come on, brain, engage. An opportunity like this wasn't going to come along very often and I couldn't afford to blow it. If he was going to choose me over Vanessa, I had to be witty and charming and original.

"So, how long have you been going to Spencer?"

So much for original. All my insides cringed at once, but I kept the smile on my face.

And, miracle of miracles, he answered me as though I hadn't just asked him the lamest question in the world.

"Since ninth grade. Everyone in my mom's family has always gone here. My mom, my aunts and uncles, my grandma, her dad. You know."

"But did you want to? What if you'd wanted to go somewhere else?" I couldn't imagine my mom taking it for granted what school I went to and not even talking it over with me.

He shrugged. "I didn't." He jerked a thumb over his shoulder toward the school's front façade, which faced south. "I'm a day student. We live over there a couple of blocks. The family's been there since dirt was invented. I never thought about it much."

"Wow. I can't imagine one family living in one house for all those years. My dad is such a nomad, we've lived all over the place. He's a director," I added, in case he thought Dad was a traveling salesman or something.

Callum lifted an eyebrow. "Mansfield? Your dad is Gabe Mansfield?"

While my heart said, *He knows your name!,* my brain said, *He knows your dad's name!*

Give the man an A on both counts.

I nodded modestly, as though I had anything to do with it.

I swear, that smile had to have been designed by God to slay the female heart. It was a delicious triangle, with the kind of full lower lip you wanted to lean across and kiss, and the warmth in his eyes just added to it.

Bliss.

"Wow," he said. "He's one of the best directors in the business."

"Most people don't follow directors' careers," I said. I needed to focus. "Stars, yes, but not producers and directors, unless they're Spielberg or Bruckheimer."

"They do if they're planning on it for a career."

Aha. "Maybe I can introduce you to my dad sometime," I offered, oh-so-casually. "He's working in Marin for at least the next year."

"Marin? You mean at the Ranch?"

I nodded. My estimation of him rose another notch, even though there's nothing else out in Marin except cows and houses, so it was a pretty easy guess. "He and George are doing a joint project. So Dad will probably drop in here for events and stuff."

"Yeah?" Again the smile flashed, and again I went down for the count. I'd make my dad adopt him if that's what it took to produce that smile.

Ew, rewind. That would make him my adoptive brother, and totally not what I had in mind. Maybe I could ask Dad to hire Callum as an intern.

"Benefactors' Day is in October," he told me. "It's a big hoo-hah where we all show off, and in the evening there's a charity ball in the assembly hall. It used to be a ballroom. People shell out a thousand a plate, and the proceeds go to whatever charity or foundation is kissing up to Curzon that week."

He'd lost me at "charity ball." In my imagination, I saw myself in the absolute knockout dress of the century (note to self: find first weekend available for shopping trip to L.A.), dancing with Callum McCloud in front of an envious crowd, at the front of which was an abandoned and jealous Vanessa Talbot. All around me, teachers and parents wondered who the beautiful creature was, and every boy in tenth grade and up wished he could date me. But I was oblivious to it all, looking up into Callum's eyes and—

"—go to before?"

Callum's voice penetrated the oohs and ahhs of the imaginary crowd. I came back to earth with a thump and a red face.

"Sorry, Callum. I spaced for a second there. What did you say?"

"I just asked you what school you went to before."

I told him, leaving out the part about Aidan Mitchell and my former best friend, the homecoming queen. *Mo guai nuer* that she was.

My first week at a new school and I was already speaking Mandarin. Mom would be so proud. She's big into diversity.

Callum gestured, and I realized that once again I'd zoned out on him. How was that possible? We were getting to know each other. If I was going to be the one in his arms at the Benefactors' Day charity ball, I needed to pay attention to everything he said. Make him feel he was important to me, in a non-stalkerish way. And that would make me important to him.

I made some innocuous comment, which seemed to kill the conversation. Now that we'd exhausted what Dad called the "tombstone information" about ourselves, I wanted more.

I wanted to get personal. To make him open up a little about the things that mattered to him. After that e-mail from my sister, I wanted to be able to give her the right answer to her question.

I opened my mouth to say something witty and charming and original, when something whacked my shoulder. Something large and heavy and knobby.

"Oops," Vanessa said, rounding the corner of the table and sitting in the chair next to Callum. She set her large, heavy, knobby backpack on the floor and turned her brown eyes with their sixties retro mascara on him. Perfectly smooth hair swung. "Sorry I'm late. Ready?"

"Sure." He gathered up his notebook and textbooks and slid them into his own backpack. "Nice talking to you, Melissa."

"It's Lissa," I said automatically.

Two facts had detonated in my head. One was that, while I had been thinking we were developing the first levels of a soul connection, he had just been killing time until Vanessa showed up.

And two, now she knew that I was interested.

DLavigne   Poacher alert! Melissa moving in on C RIGHT NOW. Library.

VTalbot   Already handled.

DLavigne   I can't believe her.

VTalbot   I can. Only a blonde wouldn't figure out he's not available.

DLavigne   Supper looks vomit-inducing. TouTou's 7pm?

VTalbot   Lucy & Lily custom-made capris came today. Perfect timing :) Tell Emily.

DLavigne   OK. Photogs at the gate. Go out by the field house.

VTalbot   OK, tx.

chapter 6

'M CONVINCED THAT humiliation is visible. I stayed in the
library, pretending to look for a book, waiting for my hot face to
cool, until the gong sounded and it was time for my next class.
On my way down the hall, I passed a bulletin board and there it
was. Already.

Christian Prayer Circle
Tuesday nights at 7:00 p.m.
Room 216
Bibles not necessary, but bring yours if you want.
First circle forms tonight!

Gillian hadn't wasted any time. When had she made that
poster, found the neon-pink paper, and printed it? And starting
tonight? Couldn't she have given me a couple of days to get used
to the idea?

Because of course I was going. I could do that without advertising to the whole world that I was a Christian. Spencer was thick with associations and groups and societies, so one more wouldn't even be a blip on the radar. Besides, it wasn't like Vanessa and the crew were going to be there. It hadn't been me in the halls, putting up bright pink notices. I was safe.

When I walked into the dining room for lunch, the first thing I saw was Gillian at a table on one side, holding court with some kind of story. I didn't know her as well as I was going to, but even then I knew that her stories were true. A girl as committed to Christ as Gillian was simply didn't make things up. This time the soundtrack on her CD player was Rebecca St. James's brand-new album. Whether the other students knew it or not, Christian music was filtering into their subconscious.

Ah, the subtlety of the east. As in New York. What did you think I meant?

Between chowing down our lunch and the story (which turned out to be the one about the elevator in the Eiffel Tower, minus the music by the Jangle person), I didn't get a chance to talk to Gillian alone until we were heading back to our room to get our books for the afternoon.

"I see the posters are up," I said. "How'd you do it so fast? You only came up with the idea this morning."

"Did you know we have our own print shop?" she asked by way of a reply. "I asked at the office where I could print them, and they told me to go to the basement, where they print the school paper. They have computers and scanners and everything there. And with two classroom wings times three floors times two bulletin boards each, I was only late for AP Chem by ten minutes." She paused. "I got detention, but it was worth it."

Harsh. "You? Who gives detention for being late?"

She shot me a rueful glance. "Milsom. Some of the kids at lunch told me he's Mr. Anal when it comes to starting class on time."

"I'm so not looking forward to Chem next year. Apparently he's Mr. Anal about everything, like wiping down the lab and neutralizing all the surfaces at the end of every class."

Out of all our classes, we only had Global Studies together. English is pretty fun, but Gillian is a math and science girl. I help her with her essays, and she helps me with the mental agony that is sine and cosine and the cellular makeup of, well, anything.

"I like my lab partner, though," Gillian went on. "Her name's Carly Aragon and she seems really nice."

"Aragon." I remembered the name from roll call, only because that was the name of Henry the Eighth's first queen. "She's in U.S. History with me, I think. Same height as you, long curly brown hair?"

"That's her. I invited her to the prayer circle."

"Of course you did."

"Who'd *you* invite?"

"Well, considering I didn't know it was starting tonight until after free period, no one."

I opened my mouth to tell her about Callum, and then closed it again. She'd been pretty blasé about him last night, and I didn't feel like inviting any more of it while I was still feeling flattened over him and Vanessa. Chances were she'd hear about them being a couple before the end of the day, and I could just let the whole subject die a quiet death.

I'd do my mourning in private.

Supper turned out to be broiled salmon and *haricots verts*. Clearly the administration was no slouch in the nutrition department. That's one thing about Spencer—with the exception of the oatmeal in the morning, the food here is really good. Of course, for the tuition, I guess it ought to be. So I downed my omega-threes and went upstairs to get ready for prayer circle.

"How are you going to organize this?" I asked Gillian as I pulled a handmade Aran cable-knit sweater over my T-shirt (empty of slogans, per the aforementioned rule) and my faded-to-a-sigh Citizens of Humanity jeans. Outside of class hours, we could throw on pretty much whatever we wanted, thank goodness. You can only go so many hours in a day in a plaid skirt and a buttoned-up white blouse.

Not to mention knee socks or navy tights. Gack.

"What's to organize?" she asked me. Juicy cargo pants and a tank top were a good look for her. She has no hips, unlike some of us. "After everybody gets there, we take turns praying. Then we go out for coffee or something. There's a Starbucks on the corner of the next block."

"Sounds good. I hope people show up."

Room 216 in the classroom wing looked as though it had been a student lounge once, but the art department had turned it into a miniature gallery. A big Chinese dragon shared wall space with a humanoid face with pins in its eyes. I turned my back on it and faced the half dozen people who were standing around.

"Hey," Gillian said with a smile that lit up her face. "Welcome to our first prayer circle. Thanks for coming."

"What are we praying for?" said a thin guy who was tall enough to try out for basketball, if Spencer played in any competitive leagues. Which it didn't, except for, of all things, rowing and golf. Why would rich kids want to do something where they might actually be required to sweat?

"Anything you want. God's not fussy."

"I'm not praying to any icon of a male-focused hierarchy," a girl with blue hair informed Gillian. "I'll pray to the Goddess. The circle is her symbol."

Gillian waved her hands as if to dispel this idea before it got a chance to land. "The notice said this is a Christian prayer circle. Our prayers go to God only."

The girl looked at her as though she were completely deluded. "I'm out of here, then."

The tall boy followed her. That left a girl whom I belatedly realized was Carly Aragon, Gillian's chem partner, and two boys, neither of whom I knew. Yet. Prayer tends to get you acquainted with people in a hurry.

"Let's start," Gillian said. "We should join hands and—"

The door opened. "Is this the prayer circle?" somebody asked, and giggled.

Oh, no. I knew that giggle.

Vanessa, Emily, and Dani stepped in, with Callum and Brett Loyola right behind them. Say what you want, but I just didn't have a whole lot of faith that they were there to get close to God.

Gillian didn't even blink. "Come on in and join us."

Emily and Dani looked at each other like this was a huge joke, and Emily giggled again. "I'm going to pray for you," Dani told her. "You so totally need it."

"What about you? You need it worse than me."

"It wasn't me in the girls' bathroom—"

"Okay, okay, shut up," Vanessa told them. She looked over at Gillian and me. "So. You guys are Christians?"

"Yes," Gillian said. She's fearless.

"Yes," I said. I'm truthful. When I'm cornered.

The two boys looked at each other, looked at Brett and Callum, and just sort of melted out of the room. Sheesh. They needed a dose of the Old Testament. You know, be strong and courageous and go out and smite the enemy and all that.

So with Carly, who still hadn't said a word, that left the three of us against five, but as I said before, Gillian is fearless. "Okay, we're going to join hands, go around and tell each other our names in case we don't know them, and then I'll pray first."

"What are you going to pray for?" Dani asked. "Moo goo gai pan?"

"If I were hungry, I might," Gillian said evenly. "But since I'm not, I'll pray for something important."

"Like getting Brett a date?" Vanessa laughed and squeezed Brett around the waist with one arm, as if they'd been best friends since babyhood. Maybe they had. I glanced at Callum for his reaction, but he was just watching her indulgently, as though anything she did was just fine with him.

"No, but I'd pray for him if he had a real problem, like his homework was getting him down because he was illiterate or his friends were making him angry by being idiots."

Okay, clearly Gillian was reaching her limit.

"Are you calling me an idiot?" Vanessa inquired in a tone so silky you just knew things were about to get rough.

"I was speaking hypothetically," Gillian said.

"I don't like being called an idiot, even hypothetically," Vanessa told her. "You can apologize now."

"For what? Using a literary device?" I asked, jumping in with both loafers.

Vanessa stared at me. She didn't get it. Not that a little thing like an allusion would stop her. "I'm a little surprised to see you here. I didn't think you were all that righteous."

"I'm not."

"I know. Poacher."

I felt my skin go cold.

"Look at her," she said to Dani. "Is that a guilty face or what?"

"What are you guys talking about?" Callum's voice was either lazy or bored.

I swear my blood stopped in my veins. If she told him I was crushing on him in front of everybody, I would just shrivel up and have to transfer to some school in the Central Valley where no one would ever know my name.

And Vanessa knew it. Triumph, and the knowledge that she

could blackmail me anytime she wanted, sparkled in her eyes. And it seemed to satisfy her. Or maybe she didn't want Callum to clue in to the fact that there were more interesting fish in the aquarium than her. Whatever. The point is, she left that arrow alone and picked up the sling she'd arrived with.

"So go on," she said. "I want to see you pray."

"You're not supposed to watch it; you're supposed to *do* it," Gillian said.

"Do Christian girls do it?" Brett Loyola asked no one in particular.

"Hey, now," Callum said. Why was it that I could never tell what he meant? Was he warning Brett to keep it clean, or was he acknowledging a new idea? Whose side was he on?

Then again, I wasn't sure I wanted confirmation.

Whatever he meant, it was too late. "Oh, good question," Vanessa said. "If I join your prayer circle, do I have to be a virgin?"

"I hope not." Emily giggled. That sound was really beginning to annoy me.

"Are all Christian girls virgins?" Dani wanted to know.

Gillian looked at me, and Carly looked at her. We needed to do something, and fast. The absolute last thing any of us wanted was to have a discussion of our sex lives (or lack thereof) anywhere within a hundred miles of this bunch.

"In answer to your question, no, you don't have to be a virgin to be in the prayer circle," Gillian said out of the last reserves of her patience. "You just have to be sincere. Now, are you guys sincere, or are you just here to be obnoxious?"

"Oh, we're sincere, all right," Dani said. "We sincerely think you guys are pathetic. Dear God, make him like me," she whined. "He's so cu-u-u-te."

Gillian closed her eyes, and in her I'm-telling-a-story-in-a-noisy-dining-room voice, said, "Father, thank You for bringing us all together this evening. Thank You for Your Son, who was willing to die for us so we could come together in Your Spirit and talk with You. I pray that You would whack—uh, work on certain people so they'd approach You with respect. Bless the—"

"Come on, Cal," Brett said. "This is way too serious for me."

Callum nodded, and he and Brett loped out of the room. Dani and Emily looked as though they might go, too, but Vanessa put a hand on Dani's arm.

"Bless the students here at Spencer, and open their eyes to Your beauty," Gillian went on. "We pray You'd open up the gospel to us as we study Your Word. Be with—"

"Gospel?" Dani said. "Isn't that like what Honey Do sings?"

I had no clue who Honey Do was, but it didn't sound good. Some hip-hop star, maybe?

"No, dummy," Emily said. I bet she was happy that, for once, she knew something that the other two didn't. "The gospel is, like, the Bible."

"It's not the Bible. It means 'good news,'" Carly said quietly, surprising all of us. It was the first time she'd opened her mouth.

"And how would you know that, MexiDog?"

Laughing as if this was the biggest joke in the world, they gave it up and flounced out into the hall, singing, "Jesus loves me, this I know, 'cuz my girlfriend's such a ho," at the tops of their voices.

"Give it a *rest*," Carly said.

The off-key sound of this charming ditty moved off down the hall in the direction of the girls' dorm.

When finally we couldn't hear them anymore, Gillian looked from me to Carly. "Well?" she said wearily. "Want to have a prayer triangle?"

Carly looked uncomfortable. "I—I'm not really sure."

I leaned over and took Gillian's hand, then Carly's. Her fingers were icy cold. Gillian took Carly's other hand to close our triangle, and I shut my eyes.

"Father, I have only one thing to ask," I said into the quiet. "Please help us get through junior year."

"Amen," all three of us said.

Together.

You'd almost think it had been planned.

....

✉

To: kazg@hotmail.com
From: lmansfield@spenceracad.edu
Date: September 24, 2008
Re: Re: How ya doin'?

Hey Kaz,

Thanks for the note. I really miss PHS. Way more than I thought. Any chance you could transfer up here? They have a great graphic arts department. Haha. Pacific Heights probably isn't ready for graphic novels about spiritual warfare. Have you sent DEMON BATTLE out to publishers yet?

No boyfriends, but there are a few possibles. You were right about Aidan. I promise I will listen to you next time.

I have a great roomie named Gillian Chang. Picture Katie Leung in cargo pants with a New York accent and an attitude the size of the Statue of Liberty. And she's a Christian! Remind me to tell you about THAT next time I'm home. Oy. My head hurts thinking about it. And a girl called Carly Aragon came to our first prayer circle. Brave girl. I think she's a believer but I'm not sure.

Not a lot of us around here. I feel like an alien in a cage with people poking sticks through the bars. Ooh, look at the pretty green Christian. Sigh. Any advice?

Love, Lissa xoxo

chapter 7

MAYBE I COULD become a day student, and commute from Marin.

On Friday I skipped breakfast and got a yogurt from the machine instead, then hid out in core class (Reading the British Canon), where I knew no one. Well, after a couple of days of roll call, I knew names and some faces, but what I mean is that no one from Tuesday's debacle was in sight.

Being a Christian wasn't supposed to be this hard. At PHS, you were what you were and people just got over it. Or maybe, I thought suddenly, that was just how I saw it from inside my crowd. We were what we were . . . and everyone wanted to be like us.

Here, I was on the outside, and by default, that meant people were free to judge me. To my face and behind my back.

I hate that.

Okay, so probably you do, too. But the little baby inside me was still crying, *Like me! Like me!* and not getting what she wanted.

The flat-panel display on the wall changed from the nine

o'clock CNN news feed to a close-up of Ms. Curzon, who held a sheaf of paper. Most schools have announcements over the P.A. system. At Spencer, you have plasma and CNN.

"Good morning, ladies and gentlemen," Ms. Curzon began. (I think she's trying to give us positive reinforcement by referring to us that way.) "It's Friday, the twenty-sixth of September, and the first full week of classes is nearly behind us. I hope you're all settling in, making new friends, and finding new activities to enjoy.

"On that last subject, signups for the Christmas play are posted outside the drama department. Ms. Chepstow tells me you'll be presenting a modern-day version of *Persuasion*. Practice for the intramural volleyball and soccer teams will be at the field house at two today, and tryouts for the gymnastics and golf teams at four. Day students, that includes you. Our golf coach, Mr. Reynolds, wants to thank the juniors—now seniors—who stayed with the team. He hopes we will once again make the regional tournament and bring home that trophy. You may, of course, sign up for rowing and sailing on Saturday, which do not happen, as you can imagine, here on campus, but on Friday afternoons at the Tiburon Yacht Club. Details are posted at the field house."

Hm. Volleyball and soccer were cool, and I was good at both. I just had to make up my mind and commit to something. I made a note in my iPhone to ping me at one forty-five so I'd remember to go find the field house, wherever that was. Jocks didn't care what religion you were. All that mattered was whether you could blast the ball past your opponent's ear.

"Lastly, ladies and gentlemen, I'd like to announce that our annual Benefactors' Day will be on October eleventh. We take this opportunity every year to thank those who have been so generous to us, including your parents, guardians, businesses, and foundations. Specific activities will be detailed later, but for now, please know that your parents, guardians, or trustees will be our guests for the day, and the dinner and ball will be that evening. All proceeds will be going to a charity of the organizing committee's choice. If you'd like to be on the committee and earn your community service credits, please see Vanessa Talbot. Thank you, and enjoy your day."

LMansfield	Hi Daddy.
GabeMan	Hi baby. You doing OK?
LMansfield	Yes. Made some new friends. My roomie, Gillian Chang, and Carly Aragon. You'll like them.
GabeMan	Bring them out!
LMansfield	Are you in-country Oct 11? Benefactors' Day dinner/dance.
GabeMan	Stand by, checking…
GabeMan	Yes. Have to go to NY 10/13 but 10/11 OK.
LMansfield	Tell Mom I'll need a dress. First available weekend, I need to go to L.A.
GabeMan	She'll need one, too, right? Oh the thrill.
LMansfield	Gotta go to second period. Love you.
GabeMan	Love you 2X.

I kept an eye out for Callum all morning, but unfortunately I didn't have Math on Fridays. (I know, consider the irony of that statement.) With the prospect of meeting my dad held in reserve, I might have a chance of moving him past Tuesday's humiliation and on to happier topics, like getting to know each other as real people.

But, for once, my heat-seeking radar failed me, and when the last gong of the morning rang and I still hadn't seen him, I was forced to conclude that maybe he'd decided to skip classes and take off for the day with his friends. Fridays were dedicated to

Phys. Ed. and getting a head start on the weekend. In a couple of months, when it snowed in the Sierras, you'd need to leave at noon to have a hope of getting out to the ski hills before dinner. In the summer, it's a four-hour drive. Add winter weather and half a million people on the same highway? You do the math.

When I got back to our room after Life Science and Health to dump off my books, Gillian was just leaving for the dining room for lunch. She sat on her bed to wait while I did a fast check in the mirror and brushed my hair.

"Are you trying out for anything?" I asked. "I was thinking about soccer. Do you play volleyball?"

She waggled a hand, *etsi ketsi*. "Team sports give me hives. Gymnastics, maybe. Or how about sailing? The handbook says the school keeps a bunch of fifteen-footers at the yacht harbor."

I stared at her, brush still in my hand. "You read the handbook?"

"Didn't you? Being the authority on the dress code and all. How else are you supposed to know about stuff?"

"I ask you." I grinned at her. "And I only looked at the clothes part. I don't know about sailing. You have to take a bus to get there. Too far away."

Which, of course, was lame. I really wanted to find out what Callum was going to be doing, and until then, my decision was up in the air.

"It could be fun," she wheedled. "Come on, Lissa. Think about the wind in your hair and the tiller under your hand, smelling salt spray. . . ."

"Think about the detangler I'll need, not to mention massive sunblock. If I wanted wind and salt spray, I'd go surfing." I hated to disappoint anyone, but if I were going to hop into forty-degree ocean water, it would be with neoprene and my longboard. "I'll stick to soccer for now."

"Mud up to your knees, and bruises. I can tell you're all about the glamour. Are you quite done? I'm starving."

The Spencer equivalent of dress-down Friday is Dining Services dishing up hamburgers and fries for lunch. Do you hear me complaining? I loaded mine up with lettuce and tomato and bacon strips and, for a few seconds, imagined myself back at the Burger Bar in Santa Barbara, licking ketchup off my fingers and tasting my coconut sunblock and dried saltwater.

"What's the matter?" Gillian wanted to know. Today she hadn't come prepared with a story and a soundtrack, though a couple of sophomores had perched at the end of our table with their lunches and the Friday edition of the *San Francisco Good Times,* looking like they hoped the show was about to start.

"Nothing," I said around a big mouthful. Good burger. Points to Dining Services.

Carly brought her tray over and sat next to me as Gillian said, "You looked like you were about to cry."

I shrugged, feeling a little stupid to be caught having a moment in a place as public as this. "My burger made me homesick for a second, that's all."

She blinked at me. "Your burger."

"There's this place in Santa Barbara that makes them. We used to go all the time—you know, surf in the morning, eat there, and then catch a movie or something."

My life, the way it used to be. I missed it so much—Kaz, my sister, my friends—that without warning, a great big lump formed in my throat. I had to swallow it down with pineapple juice.

"Don't you guys ever get homesick?" I asked, finally.

"I'll be home for Christmas," Gillian pointed out so reasonably that I felt even sillier. "I love my family, but with three brothers, the parents, and my grandmother all in one apartment, sharing a room with just you is a relief."

The whole family in one apartment? I pictured Chinatown and noise and cartons of vegetables in the storefront downstairs and the smells of half a dozen hole-in-the wall restaurants in the same block. *How does her family afford to send her to Spencer?* I wondered, and then reminded myself it was none of my business. They'd gone to Paris, too. Maybe there was money in the food industry.

"My dad's in San Jose, so he's only sixty miles away," Carly offered, pulling a bacon strip out of her burger and eating it. "But sometimes it feels like he's in another state."

"Where's your mom?" I asked her.

"In Mexico, with my grandparents. They're divorced."

Oh. Open mouth, insert foot. "I'm sorry."

She shrugged. "Dad has custody of me and my little brother. We do okay. But he travels a lot with his job. Computers, you know? Antony is in boarding school, too. It's just easier this way."

My mom spent most of her week in Los Angeles, working, but at least we had the option of all being together on the weekends. Poor Carly.

"There are boarding schools in San Jose, aren't there?" Gillian asked around a mouthful of alfalfa sprouts.

"Maybe. But Dad wanted me here. And it worked out with"— Carly hesitated—"admissions and everything."

I glanced at her. I'd have bet the rest of my burger that wasn't what she'd started to say.

"I bet God wants both of us here." Gillian's tone held absolute conviction.

"How do you know?" Carly asked.

She smiled. "Because you're not in Silicon Valley and I'm not at Choate or some other East Coast school. I wanted to do something different, so I asked God about it, and doors started opening right and left. Did you know this place has music scholarships?"

I shook my head. The number of things I didn't know astonished me.

"Well, it does. And I got one. For piano."

I remembered the harp and wondered what it was for. A design element?

"A music scholarship. Who knew?" she went on. "My dad was expecting math or maybe science, but hey, I'm not fussy. The point is, I figure God wants me out here for a reason, so here I am."

"I don't know what He wants me here for." I stabbed a fry into the paper cup of ketchup, conveniently forgetting to mention that I'd chosen Spencer. I'd had options, but I'd put myself right here on purpose. "Other than to provide endless entertainment for Vanessa."

Carly looked uncomfortable, but Gillian just came out with it. "You're obsessed with her."

"I am not! Is Luke obsessed with Darth Vader? No. He just wants to stay alive."

Gillian looked at Carly. "Not to mention that she has definite image problems."

"That was a metaphor." I stood and piled my empty burger wrapper and juice container on my tray. "I've got to go."

"Later."

I could feel their gazes between my shoulder blades as I left the dining room. Gillian had no filters. Did she say whatever she wanted without thinking about the other person's feelings? I was not obsessed, unless you counted the good kind of obsession, namely Callum McCloud. Nor did I have problems, image or otherwise. Sure, I wished my boobs were bigger and my hair smoother, but that was normal.

Just because I wasn't dancing with joy at all the changes I had to deal with didn't make me obsessive, or unhappy with God, or whatever Gillian was implying.

I was still fuming about it as I crossed the lawn, looking for someone who would tell me where the field house was. So naturally, I didn't even notice Callum McCloud coming up behind me until his shoulder bumped mine.

chapter 8

M Y HEART and my breathing stopped for a full second, I swear.

So did my brain. This is what happens when it doesn't get blood and oxygen. And you thought I wasn't paying attention in Biology, didn't you? I sucked in a breath, and all systems resumed operation. Oh, man, Callum smelled good. Euphoria, I was sure of it.

So apropos.

"Hey," he said, and one side of his mouth quirked up in a way that made my brain blank again.

"Hey." Again, not original, but it was the best I could do.

"Heading for the field house?"

I nodded. "I thought I'd try out for soccer. You?"

He shrugged and shook his head. "Probably sailing."

Okay, so I was going to have to backpedal with Gillian. Meanwhile, how come he was walking to the field house with me? Warm and bubbly, hope tingled through me.

"So . . . where exactly is it?"

As far as I knew, the Spencer campus was all on this same block

50

of Pacific Heights. The quadrangle of the building sat back a little from the street, with pepper and eucalyptus trees shading the front staircase and the doors. Behind it, and down the slope, were the parking lot and the basketball and tennis courts.

"Across there." Callum pointed. "It's a hike, but what are you gonna do?"

What I'd thought was a private park turned out to be the soccer field, with an Edwardian stone building that was the field house. I learned later that it also housed an Olympic-sized swimming pool, weight rooms, and squash courts. We crossed the street and I took a step toward the gate in the fencing around the field. A man in a safari jacket leaned against it, people-watching.

"No, not that way." Callum turned and picked up his pace, so that I had to skip a little to catch up.

"Where are we going?"

"There's another gate. I can't stand those guys."

"What guys?"

"Didn't you see him? That guy on the fence was a photographer."

"He was?" I craned my neck, but we were half a block away. "Who's he waiting for?"

"Any of us. Anyone who will sell a picture. Vanessa has to deal with it all the time. Brett punched a guy out once, when he wouldn't let him go into a restaurant without posing first. I hate them. Hate that I can't have a normal life even in my own neighborhood."

"My family gets that sometimes," I offered. "Usually only when a movie comes out, though. And at premieres."

"I get it all the time. Take my advice." He glanced at me. "Stay under the radar and don't let people talk about you. Then you can keep your life to yourself."

We went through another gate and walked across the field, with me slowing my steps practically to a crawl to take as long as possible getting there. Callum didn't seem to mind—or even notice.

I had to change the subject to happier topics. This might be my only opportunity, so I needed to mine it for all it was worth.

"So I talked to my dad about the Benefactors' Day thing," I said. "He's going to be in town. I was afraid he was going to have to go to New York, but that's not 'til the Monday after."

"Yeah?"

I lost my train of thought again as those eyes met mine. Not as green as the grass we walked on. More of a willow green, with a bit of Earl Grey tea thrown in.

I took a breath. "So maybe I can introduce you then."

"That'd be great."

We were still hundreds of yards away from the field house, and the ears of a bunch of milling students. Was this my opportunity? Should I take the plunge and say, "If we went to the dance together, you could spend a lot more time talking to my dad"? Somehow that didn't sound as romantic as it could. I wanted him to do the asking. And to do it because he wanted to, not because it might get him an introduction or a summer internship.

This was about me and him, not about business.

But first, I needed to know a few things. "Is Vanessa looking forward to it?"

He looked at me curiously. "I guess. Girls like dressing up and all that."

I couldn't just come out and ask him if he was going with her. "Well, I hope she lets you have a dance with me."

Even that was pretty heavy-handed, but I couldn't think of a way around it.

"Lets me?" He huffed a laugh.

"Well, you know. Some people expect their date to stick with them the whole evening."

"She's not going with me." He sounded surprised that I would think that.

I turned my biggest smile on him. "Oh? But I thought—"

"I've known Vanessa my whole life," he said. "We hang out."

Oh joy oh joy oh—

"If I asked her to the dance, she'd laugh at me. We don't stick around anyway. Brett usually throws a party, or I do."

This was a good news/bad news scenario. The good news was, he wasn't Vanessa's date, and he wasn't likely to be. The bad news was, it didn't sound like he was too inclined to ask anybody else, either.

A private party was better anyway. My task was clear. No matter what, I was going. As of this moment, I was renewing my goal to become best friends with Vanessa, Dani, and Emily.

We were only a few hundred feet from the crowd now. "A bunch of us are going down to San Gregorio beach on Sunday," Callum said. "You doing anything?"

Sunday. Sunday. I pulled out my iPhone. Church and lunch with my parents. My dad's not a believer, but my mom . . . well, she goes to church when she has time. We'd had this on the calendar since she'd kissed me good-bye at my dorm the week before. She'd spin over in the Mercedes and get me, we'd go to this tiny little clapboard church she'd found by Googling "church Marin County," and then the three of us would have lunch at whatever her latest favorite place was. Some people have a nose for fine diamonds or the latest designers. My mom has a nose for food. Put her down in a Hungarian village and she'll find the best place to eat in ten minutes or less.

"Oh, man," I said, "I'm supposed to spend Sunday with my parents."

"They won't mind, will they?"

I haven't seen them for a week. And getting them both in one place at the same time is a miracle. No, I couldn't say that. It would make me sound like I was nine years old. But I wanted to see them. I wanted to drag Gillian over to Marin and watch her make my dad laugh.

At the same time, the thought of spending a day at the beach, of watching Callum take his shirt off, of borrowing a board from someone and catching a wave . . .

This was *so* not fair.

"Can I come next time?" I smiled playfully at him. "I'd love to go."

"Sure," he said. "I guess you're right. If I had the chance to spend the day with your dad, I probably would, too."

I opened my mouth to invite him, dumping Gillian off my mental calendar, but at that moment a group of guys hailed him. He smiled at me and loped off, leaving me to find my way into the soccer group on my own.

Loss sat in my chest like a dead weight. Loss of opportunity, loss of time with Callum. From here on out, I told myself, I wasn't going to make plans. Maybe he wouldn't ask me again. Some guys had such fragile egos they could only handle "no" once. Turn them down and they never come back. Callum didn't strike me that way—a guy as popular as he was couldn't be that fragile—but you never knew. He could have sensitive depths to him that I would have to handle carefully.

He'd see. I'd be the best girlfriend he ever had.

LMansfield	Hey Mom.
Patricia_Sutter	There you are.
LMansfield	OK if I bring my roomie Sunday?
Patricia_Sutter	Of course. Pick you up at 9:30.
Patricia_Sutter	I'm in L.A. You should go see your dad tomorrow. He'd love to have you to himself.
LMansfield	Sorry, I can't. Phys. Ed. signups.
Patricia_Sutter	Oh right. See you Sunday.
Patricia_Sutter	Love you.
LMansfield	Love you 2X.

chapter 9

GILLIAN LOOKED a little surprised on Saturday morning when the bus chartered to take us to the yacht club pulled up and I got on it with her.

"What's up with you?"

I shrugged. "I thought I'd give sailing a try. It isn't surfing, but you made it sound like fun."

And then Callum got on the bus, along with Vanessa, Dani, Brett, and Todd. Gillian gave me a look, rolled her eyes, and pulled her iPod out of her backpack. She settled back for the ride and didn't give the others another glance.

I, on the other hand, knew exactly the moment when Callum looked away from whatever Dani had been saying to him. We rolled down the hill past the house where the exteriors for *Mrs. Doubtfire* were shot, and I turned my head. Our gazes connected, and his eyes crinkled in a not-quite smile that told me he was glad I was there.

Warmth flooded my body and I struggled with the dopey smile that wanted to paste itself all over my face. I settled for a flicker of my lashes and turned to look outside again.

Gillian elbowed me and took one of her earphones out. "If you don't want to crew with me, let me know now."

"Of course I'll crew with you."

"Even if you get a better offer?"

"I'm not taking sailing lessons for that."

"Huh," she said in a tone that painted me totally transparent.

"Besides, Va—those guys would probably make sure we capsized if I was on the boat."

"And you still want these people to be your friends?"

"Just some of them. My real friends come and meet my family."

Gillian smiled at me and the little suspicious coolness that had seemed to fog our view of each other dissipated in the warmth.

"You meant what you said at breakfast, right? I mean, I could look up a local church and go on my own. No biggie."

"I meant it." I pushed aside the memory of how easily I'd been prepared to ditch her if it had meant Callum coming to lunch instead. It had only been a thought. Easy come, easy go. No harm done.

Except that if his friends hadn't interrupted, I might have done a little harm. How would I have felt if Gillian had made plans with me and then ditched me the first time some guy smiled at her?

Was I really that desperate for new friends, and Callum in particular, that I would become the kind of person I despised?

Ouch.

I needed to stop thinking about that before I started asking Gillian's forgiveness for something I hadn't even done.

The bus rolled past a sign that said Tiburon Yacht Club, and I straightened up as Gillian put her stuff away. You might think that sailing at the end of September is just asking to be swamped by a fall storm, but the truth is, it was over eighty and clear outside as we trooped out of the bus.

My lime-green and black Body Glove zip-top halter and mini

were what I usually wore when I went out on friends' boats or catamarans in S.B. But up here, it was different. Callum wore jeans. Vanessa had on capris that fit as though they'd been tailor-made for her, with D&G strawberry-colored deck shoes. Didn't they expect to get wet? I mean, you didn't have to fall in. There'd be plenty of spray to go around.

The instructor couldn't have been more than twenty-five, and whoa, was he gorgeous. Shaggy blond hair with that laid-back vibe of a guy who spent all his time caring about wind direction and not much else. Cushy job. Kaz should get a gig like this while he tried to get *Demon Battle* published.

"Guys. Ladies," he greeted us as we gathered in a crowd on the dock next to a row of upended hulls. "I'm Jake Mercer, and I'll be your sailing instructor for the next ten weeks. Except for today, of course, we'll meet on Fridays, same time. You'll be starting out on fifteen-foot Coronados crewed by two each, and at week five you'll progress to twenty-four-foot Moores crewed by four. Your final consists of nothing more than a sail to Treasure Island and back without running into a ferry, a bridge, or some kind of land mass."

Dani and Emily giggled, and he smiled at them.

"Okay, let's get started."

After the obligatory talk about safety and the rules of the water ("Stay on the right when you make your way out of the harbor, just like driving a car"), we had to assemble a boat. Gillian and I worked up a sweat lugging the mast and sail over, stepping the mast, sliding the keel into its slot, and figuring out which ropes—which are called *sheets* for reasons that escape me—do what. I didn't expect to actually get into the water on the first day, but that shows you what I know.

Gillian looked from me to the little Coronado bobbing next to the dock. "Tell me you know how to steer one of these."

I got in and steadied it for her while she clambered aboard. "No, but I bet Jake is about to tell us."

"What do you mean? You've got the outfit. You must know."

"I've sailed on other people's boats. The most I ever had to do was find my own Diet Coke in the galley."

"Great." She was looking green already. "I'm not touching that thing."

And who'd been trying to talk *me* into it? I gripped the tiller. "That means you have to be ballast. Sit there, on the gunwale, and give us some balance. These things tilt when you get some speed going. That much I do know."

Out of the corner of my eye, I saw Brett take the tiller of the next boat and Callum wind the sheet around his hand as if he'd done it a hundred times. Their sail luffed in the breeze and then filled as they turned, and they sailed out into the channel between the docks like Sasha Cohen doing a spread eagle at the Olympics.

Men. They made it look so easy. Meantime, Gillian and I wobbled and bobbled and tilted so close to the water I could see the starfish wrapped around the pilings deep down.

Guhhh. I'd been right to want to stick to something with fewer movable parts.

Vanessa and Dani crewed the next boat, launching right behind us. And behind them, Emily sat on the gunwale chirping admiring things at Todd as he slid the keel in and pushed off from the dock.

Gillian gasped. "Lissa, we're going to hit!"

I jerked the tiller over to the left and we missed some guy's catamaran by, like, two inches. Gillian switched sides and fended it off with her bare hands until we got past. "Lawsuit averted," she muttered. "Pay attention, will ya?"

"I'm good." I gripped the tiller like a drowning person, which is what I would be if I didn't master this thing. The water tugged at the rudder, the wind tugged at the sail, and between the two of them, I was having to process way more information than usual. "Other side!"

We wobbled out into the channel, where the breeze whistled happily down the open stretch between rows of boats. Expensive boats. Boats with fiberglass hulls that could be pierced by our bow and sink, along with all their nice teak decking and designer bed coverings and state-of-the-art GPS electronics.

What kind of lunatic had said that sailing was fun? I was never laughing at Kaz's dad with his goofy captain's cap again.

"Look out!" Gillian shrieked.

Vanessa and Dani's boat bore down on us like a runaway train, only slightly more out of control than we were.

"Talbot!" Jake shouted from his boat, which he was crewing single-handed. "Come about!"

"How?" she yelled.

"Steer into the wind. Now!"

"Impact four seconds," Gillian said. She had been green before. Now she was as white as the sail that flapped uselessly above her head.

How did I steer? Where was the wind? What should I—

I stood up, letting go of the tiller and grabbing a sheet in each hand. I had some vague plan about pulling the sail tighter, about changing direction, about—

Crump.

Vanessa's boat hit ours dead amidships. The hull tilted up. Gillian grabbed the boom and hung on with both arms, and I went butt-over-Body Glove into San Francisco Bay.

chapter 10

THE COLD PARALYZED ME.

Arms, legs, face, lungs. Surfing in the Pacific in SoCal had not prepared me in any way for the frigid water only six hours' drive north. As the dark green water thundered closed over my head, all I could think about was getting *out*—and fast.

I kicked for the surface just as something plummeted into the water next to me. I had no idea what it was—I'd squeezed my eyes shut so I wouldn't lose my contact lenses. An arm reached out and snaked around my waist, and powerful legs propelled both of us to the surface. As my face broke into the air, water streaming off me and my hair tangling around my neck and arms, I heard shouting but couldn't make out the words.

"Grab the gunwale."

I pushed water out of my eyes and saw a hull looming in front of my face. I reached up and hooked my hands on the gunwale as it tilted toward me.

"Kick as hard as you can!"

I kicked, whoever it was heaved, and I shot up and over the gunwale, landing like a beached elephant seal in the bottom of the boat.

"Lissa, are you okay?" Gillian helped me roll over and sit up. Eighty degrees outside or not, the cold had gone through skin, muscle, and bone, right to my core. My teeth chattered as I tried to speak.

"Y-yeah."

"McCloud, here!"

I looked up as Jake, the instructor, leaned over the gunwale of his own boat and Callum kicked up and out of the water into it. A lot more gracefully than I just had.

Callum?!

Gillian yanked a pristine white Spencer Academy bath towel out of her backpack and wrapped it around me. "Thanks." I huddled inside the towel, which meant Gillian had to get the boat turned around and get us back to the dock all by herself.

"I can't believe it," she whispered. "Can't believe it. You should have seen him. Dove right in after you. I take back every nasty thing I ever said about him."

"He'd d-do it for anyone."

But would he?

All around us, the girls twittered and relayed what had just happened to the people who'd missed it. Jake called, "Mansfield. You okay?"

"Yes," I said, molars clacking on the word.

"Chang, get her to the wharf. We'll get her dried off and find her something hot to drink. The rest of you, the excitement's over. Practice tacking up and down this open stretch for thirty minutes, and come back in."

Reluctantly, the other boats peeled off. All except one.

Vanessa leaned over the gunwale while Dani tacked behind us and to one side. "Melissa, I'm so sorry. I didn't know how to turn and I just . . . fell apart. Are you sure you're okay?"

"It's *Lissa*. I'm okay. Just c-cold."

"We're coming back with you, just to make sure."

Given the choice of Callum, Gillian, or Vanessa making sure you were okay, who would you pick? But it was nice of her to make the gesture. I mean, with at least a dozen witnesses, she could hardly do anything else. Call me cynical, but considering the way she'd been treating me for the last week, it was pretty hard to see her running into us as an accident.

Maybe it was. Maybe she was telling the truth. Or maybe she was giving an Oscar-winning performance, white face, huge eyes, and all.

I was too cold and wet to care. And there was something long and slimy stuck to my calf. I peeled the bit of seaweed off my leg and tossed it over the side. Gillian brought the boat around so that it bumped against the dock—only hard enough to jar my teeth, not enough to send me into the water again. Not bad for her first time.

"Take my hand."

Callum materialized in front of me for the second time in five minutes. His hand was big and damp and beautiful as it engulfed mine and he helped me out of the boat and onto the dock.

"Thank you," I said fervently. "You saved my life."

His hair stuck up every which way, and water trickled down his legs to puddle in his wet deck shoes. He shrugged and looked embarrassed. "Nah. You wouldn't drown with all these people around."

"It's cold, though. Another couple of minutes and hypothermia might have set in."

"And speaking of that," Jake said, moving between us and slinging an arm around my waist, "let's get you into the boathouse, okay?"

I looked over my shoulder at Gillian, still sitting in the boat and looking a little forlorn. Jake followed my gaze. "McCloud, help Chang wash down her boat and meet us in the boathouse."

So while I got to sit in the sunny window drinking hot chocolate out of the microwave, Gillian got to do the grunt work. She and Callum unstepped the mast and rolled up the sail, tying the canvas like a big furled umbrella. Then they washed the salt and seaweed off the hull of our boat and pushed it into its place on the dock.

At least Jake was nice enough to make hot chocolate for them, too, when they came in.

"Feeling better?" Callum joined me in the window to watch Vanessa and Dani haul their boat out of the water and start scrubbing it down.

Now, there was a cheery view if I ever saw one. Almost made me want to yell, "Swab those decks, ye scurvy dogs!"

"Much," I said. Gillian sat on the bench behind him. "Thank you guys, again. They're going to be talking about this for weeks."

"I doubt it." Callum didn't seem to realize Gillian was even there. "Every term someone falls in, usually before the class where you learn how to capsize and how to get back in."

"I told you we'd be capsizing boats." I leaned over and looked at Gillian, including her in the conversation. After all, if it hadn't been for her, Callum and I would have had to swim for it, and I probably wouldn't have made it very far.

"Not 'til the ninth week." Callum leaned back and smiled at Gillian, and something inside me relaxed. I wanted my friend and my (possible future) boyfriend to be friends. After all, if they couldn't bond over my near-death experience, what was it going to take?

"Have you had this class before?" she asked.

"Oh, sure. You can take it three times for credit. During winter and spring terms I do golf. My old man plays a lot. It's about the only thing we both like."

Callum played golf with his dad? I mean, not to perpetuate a stereotype or anything, but I always saw golfers as retired guys with knee socks and plaid shorts, hauling around clubs with little fuzzy tams on them. The clubs, not the old guys.

I caught Gillian's eye and from her expression, I gathered she had the same picture. Well, weren't our stereotypes just getting knocked all over this week?

The door swung open and Vanessa and Dani burst in.

"I'm so glad you're okay!" Vanessa hugged me. With my left hand I held my paper cup of hot chocolate in the air so the impact wouldn't spill it, and with my right arm I hugged her back.

Maybe it was an act. Or maybe she really was sorry for dumping me in the bay. But if she was willing to offer the olive branch, I'd take it.

"Is there any more of that chocolate? Jake?"

My mother would have asked her if her arms were broken, but Jake just turned from organizing life jackets by size, shook a couple of packets of powder into cups, poured in water, and nuked them.

"At *our* yacht club, the chocolate is the real thing." Dani gazed at the contents of her cup like there were bug bodies floating in it. "They import it from Switzerland."

"You asked," Jake pointed out.

Dani ignored him. "So, Melissa, are you coming to San Gregorio with us tomorrow?"

"You guys, she's told you, like, twenty times that her name is *Lissa*," Gillian said.

Vanessa looked as though she hadn't noticed her until this very second. "Is it?" She glanced at me for confirmation.

"Yes. But it's okay. It doesn't matter."

"Have you been calling her Melissa?" Callum grinned at Vanessa as if he hadn't been doing the same.

"Not anymore." With a big smile, she sat on my other side. "So. San Gregorio? It's going to be fun. Bodysurfing, tanning, and the dining room's going to pack us a big lunch."

I glanced at Callum. *Pressure much?*

This is what my sister calls being stuck between a rock and

a hard place. More than anything, I wanted to go with them. I wanted to show Callum my moves on the waves, and teach him a few, if he felt like it. I wanted to take a long walk on the sand and just talk. Get to know him. Look up at his beautiful face without anyone thinking I was obsessive.

Most important of all, I wanted him to get to know me—the real me. Not the goofball falling in the water or the idiot who could never think of anything to say. Out there on the beach, where I was comfortable, surely he'd see the real me—and like me.

On the other hand . . . I sighed. A commitment was a commitment. I'd been so excited about Gillian meeting my folks. I was not going to toss that out the window for Callum.

All the same, temptation bit hard and I fought it off.

"We talked about it already," I said, shooting Callum a sideways glance. "I have plans."

"On a Sunday?" Vanessa frowned. Then her expression cleared. "Oh, I get it. You're going to church!" She looked at Dani and they both grinned.

The specter of Tuesday night loomed up in all its dark horror. I could feel Gillian's agitation from three feet away.

"You are?" Dani looked as though I'd said I was going to eat raw squid when I finished my hot chocolate. "What a waste of time."

On Callum's other side, Gillian straightened, then leaned back to catch my eye. In one look I read a whole Gospel, but she kept her mouth clamped shut.

This one was up to me.

Just what I always wanted. Taking a stand for my faith in front of the girls whose opinion mattered most at Spencer. Knowing it would be fatal.

"I don't think it's a waste of time." I answered her as if she'd said something reasonable. "Gillian's coming with my mom and me, and then we're going out to Marin for lunch."

"With your dad?" Callum asked.

"Yes, with my dad." What did he think? "We wouldn't let the poor guy starve."

He whistled, a short note of appreciation. "I still say that's worth giving up the beach for."

"What?" Dani asked.

He shot her a look. "Do you know who her dad is?"

Dani shrugged. Vanessa rolled her eyes and said, "He's a director. So what? My dad gave him money for a movie once. Big deal." She made it sound like Dad had been begging at the front door. Or maybe the servants' entrance.

"He's only one of the best directors in the business. And since she won't invite me to lunch, I guess I have to wait 'til the Benefactors' Day ball to meet him."

Oh, those eyes. Those lashes, dropping down to hood them in a way that just made my toes curl.

"Why can't he come to lunch?" Dani looked almost angry with me, as if I'd slighted Callum somehow.

"Because, dummy, then he'd have to go to church."

Vanessa has such a way with words.

"Nothing wrong with that."

Had he really said that? Or was it just wishful thinking, talking out loud in my head?

"Oh, come on," Vanessa said to him impatiently. "Your mom would faint—right after she called the guys in white coats."

"What my mom thinks is up to her," he told her in a tone devoid of expression. "I do what I want."

"You won't do that," she said with absolute conviction. "That's too out there, even for you."

"You think so?" He glanced at me. "Any chance I can hitch a ride along with you guys?"

My mouth opened, but nothing came out.

"Sure," Gillian said coolly. "Unless Lissa's mom drives a Z4. Then we'll have to tie you to the trunk."

He grinned, and the neurons in my brain fritzed out. Again. "Does she?"

"No," I managed to say. "A Mercedes."

"Great." He stood and held out his hand to me. "That means you and I can sit in the back."

LMansfield	Hey Mom.
Patricia_Sutter	Hey. I'm at my gate. Home in an hour.
LMansfield	OK if bring one more tomorrow?
Patricia_Sutter	Sure. Who?
LMansfield	You'll see.
Patricia_Sutter	A BOY????
LMansfield	Callum McCloud. Think Lauren model only blond.
Patricia_Sutter	!
Patricia_Sutter	They're calling my flight. Love you.

––––––

TRunyon	Is it true?
VTalbot	What?
TRunyon	CMcC is going to church with the princess of purity?
VTalbot	Rumor has it.
TRunyon	Way extreme. I'd do a lot to get a chick, but even I have standards.
VTalbot	You DO?

chapter 11

DRESSING FOR CHURCH isn't a big deal. At least, not in Santa Barbara. Kids come in surf shorts and T-shirts, moms come in jeans, old folks come in suits. It's all good.

But dressing for church and lunch with Callum? That's a whole different game.

The Max Azria slipdress and jacket?

Too formal. I hung it up.

The Lauren skirt and sweater set? What had I been thinking? It was so not me. That azure blue is fabulous but color isn't everything.

The D&G pants with the silk trapeze top and beautifully cut Marc Jacobs jacket?

Now we're talking.

Gillian, who had thrown on a severe black Anna Sui minidress and black tights, had been practicing on the harp for the past half hour while she waited. She stroked a rippling arpeggio and launched into something I vaguely recognized. "Please tell me you're done." She pulled perfect notes out of the air and I found myself wishing that at least some of my genes could be musical.

They aren't, and I know it, despite eight years of piano and singing lessons. This is why God gave us the iPod.

"I'm done." I put on the pearl drop necklace Dad gave me when I turned thirteen and went into the bathroom to put on my makeup.

"It's not like you need to impress this guy," she went on. "Anyone who could make comments about backseats in front of the girl who obviously wants him is already committed."

"Nobody's committed," I reminded her, stroking on mascara. "What is that you're playing?"

" 'May It Be.' From *The Lord of the Rings*."

I knew I'd heard it before. I had all the extended-version DVDs. "It's beautiful."

"Thanks. I got the lead line off the Internet and wrote my own arrangement."

Of course she did. "What's the matter with the original?"

"Nothing. I just like mine better. If you transpose it into the Dorian mode it has this great minor tone to it that—"

"Whoa! Stop. You're making my brain hurt."

She just grinned and started on the third stanza. "So do you think he's a Christian under all that bronzer and mousse?"

By this time I'd learned not to play dumb with Gillian. "He does *not* put on the pretty. Those looks are totally natural. And I don't know. If he's okay about going to church, maybe he grew up with it."

"Or maybe he just wants to meet your dad."

Cynic. I waved the pot of Urban Decay Carney lip gloss in agitation. "Has it never occurred to you that he might just like me for me? That there might not be strings attached?"

"It occurred to me." The melody shivered into silence. "But we're talking about Callum McCloud. Longtime male BFF of Vanessa Talbot. Junior Ryder Cup winner for golf. Heir to the Penoco oil fortune."

"Thank you, O queen of the research geeks. I hope you ran a criminal records check while you were at it."

"He's clean in NCIC," she informed me smugly.

I stepped out of the bathroom to stare at her. "What?"

"My cousin's husband is in the FBI. He ran a check for me last night."

"Oh, good grief." I turned and set the pot of gloss on the counter with a clack, making its little tassel jump. "That's not even legal. Or necessary. I just want to be friends. At first. I don't know how he feels."

"We'll find out, won't we? But at least you know he hasn't committed any felonies lately."

Gillian has such a way of putting everything in perspective.

Callum was already waiting outside on the front stairs when we got there. And oh, my, didn't he look fine in jeans and a white T-shirt with a rumpled Hugo Boss linen jacket over it. He had his hands jammed in his pockets against the fog that swirled around the campus, chilling everything down to sixty degrees.

Of course, he could have worn emo black with a nose ring and I'd have still thought he looked fine, not to mention completely appropriate to meet my parents.

He nodded at Gillian and smiled at me. "You look great."

I shot her a glance that plainly said, *See? Worth it, wasn't it?*

And then a diesel engine growled and a Mercedes materialized out of the fog, spitting gravel as it wheeled around the half circle of the drive. My mom understands the value of a good entrance.

Wait a second.

That wasn't her Mercedes. It was one of Dad's. And through the tinted windows I could see a man's silhouette.

My dad's personal driver, Bruno, got out of the car and opened the passenger doors. "Lissa." The guy was totally bald and built like a bear. I always wondered how he fit into anything smaller than an Escalade. Dad found him on the side of the road one day. Seriously. He was standing at an intersection holding a sign that said, "Homeless. Will drive for food." Dad, whose sense of philanthropy is a little bent, waved him over to the car, found out he'd lost his cab when he couldn't make the payments, and slid over to the passenger side. Bruno's been with us ever since.

"Bruno, where's Mom?" I tried to keep my tone even.

"Delayed in L.A."

Disappointment clogged my breathing. "But I just talked to her last night and she was at her gate."

He shrugged massive shoulders. "Apparently something came up with the campaign and the lady in charge asked her to stay over. She says she'll be here in time for lunch."

What stupid fundraising problem that could be solved in an evening there couldn't be solved over the phone from here? Arghh! She was always doing this. Always putting her charities and fundraisers and do-gooding ahead of things that were important.

Ahead of our family.

Ahead of me.

Tears burned in my eyes and I blinked, feeling my contacts float dangerously out of place with the flood of saline.

Ooooh, how I wished I could swear.

Bruno wasn't finished. "I'm supposed to take you to church and then over to the house. Are you and your friends ready?"

The damp fog had found its way through my clothes. I shivered. No, I wasn't ready. Who was ever ready to be dumped by her own mother?

"That's okay, Bruno. I'll pass." I glanced at Callum. "I had another invite, so I'll just do that instead."

"What?" Gillian blurted, gawking at me. "What invite?"

"You mean the beach?" Callum asked.

"Think they've left yet?"

"I don't think they're even out of bed."

"Perfect." I smiled at him. "I have lots of time to change, then."

"Wait a minute," Gillian said, her eyebrows lowering to make a unibrow across her forehead. Not a good look for her. "What about the service? You can deal however you want with your parents, but I still want to go to church."

I looked over at Bruno, still patiently waiting. "Bruno, do you mind taking Gillian to church on your way back over the bridge?"

"Not at all."

Bruno never minded doing anything our family asked him. He'd even gone and gotten tampons for me when I was thirteen and doubled over with the unexpected agony of cramps. Whatever my dad paid him, it wasn't enough.

"No, no." Gillian wasn't done. "We're not going to do this. What about Callum? Now he's not going to get to meet your dad."

"He'll meet him at Benefactors' Day," I said. Why the sudden concern?

"And maybe something will come up then, too. Come on, Lissa. So your mom said she'd be here this morning. Stop acting like a baby, and stick with the plan."

"*What?*" Who was she to go running me down in front of Callum like I was five years old?

"You heard me."

I opened my mouth to say something absolutely scathing, but she turned to Callum. "What do you want to do?"

He looked uncomfortable, glancing between me and Gillian. "I'm good either way."

"I bet you are," she said. "It's a win-win for you. But it's not for me." She took me by the arm and pulled me a couple of feet away. "Please, Lissa. So your mom flaked. It's not the end of the world. It just means we really need the Spirit right now, okay?"

"*You* need the Spirit," I hissed. "Where do you get off calling me a baby in front of him?"

"I'm sorry I said that." Her dark eyes told me she meant it, and I felt a little bit better. "Even if it's true, my timing is lousy."

I felt slightly less better.

"Please." Could she be any more persistent? "Let's do what we said we were going to do. Don't dump me for those guys and send me off with a driver like I'm nobody."

Ouch.

My contacts settled into place and I realized what I'd almost done. My mother had chosen something else over me. And I'd nearly chosen someone else over Gillian. Again.

Like mother, like daughter.

What right did I have to get mad at her? I wasn't a baby. I was a big fat hypocrite.

"You're right." I slipped an arm around her shoulders and gave her a squeeze. "I hate that about you. Let's go to church."

As he held the door for Callum and me to slip into the backseat, I could swear Bruno was smiling.

chapter 12

WITH BRUNO AT THE WHEEL, we shot past the photographers at the gate (did I miss a U.N. speech?) before they could even focus their lenses, and made record time winding through the emptiness that is downtown San Francisco on a Sunday morning. But if you asked me if I admired the orange arcs of the Golden Gate Bridge rearing way above us as we crossed it, or if I thought Marin was pretty, you wouldn't get much of an answer.

My whole being was focused on Callum next to me. In the front, Gillian and Bruno talked while I pretended to throw in an interested comment once in a while. Meantime, I casually let my hand fall from my lap to the foot or so of leather upholstery between us, flattening it there so it looked like I was bracing for the curves in the road.

Transparent? Yeah, maybe.

But it wasn't like he hadn't been throwing hints like Frisbees.

And then it happened. He moved his hand and linked his pinkie finger with mine.

A wave of heat and triumph and nervousness washed over me.

It was like attempting the Pipe on Oahu and washing out, but oh, man, what a ride. I'd never realized before just how many nerve endings there are in your pinkie—and every one of them was going "ooooh" at the touch of his.

Gillian glanced back, her mouth open to say something to me.

Her gaze dropped. Held.

She sat facing the windshield again, and I got a view of her profile as she spoke. "So, Callum, are you a believer?"

"In what?" His voice was as lazy as if we were all stretched out by the pool, half asleep in the sun.

"In God. We *are* on our way to church."

"I never gave it much thought."

"Do you think you might this morning?" Each word came out bright and friendly, like the plinking of piano keys. Talk about transparent.

"Maybe." The guy was unflappable. "Does it matter to you?"

"What happens to the friends of my friends matters to me."

Nine people out of ten would have asked what happens, and I could tell Gillian was just waiting to tell him. But Callum, obviously, was the tenth person.

"That's nice of you." And then he smiled at me.

Gillian rolled her eyes and subsided into her seat, and then we arrived.

I was just as glad. Gillian's passion about her faith can be a little overwhelming until you get to know her. I didn't think Callum was quite ready for it yet.

The church was one of those cute little clapboard ones painted white, with a single steeple. They're a dying breed out here in the west, which tends to run to practical concrete, unless you count the old missions. And as for the sermon the pastor gave—well, I can't tell you much about it. What was the matter with me? Even sitting next to That Jerk Aidan in church hadn't had this effect on me—this feeling that I was inside a dream, that the only thing that had any substance was the guy beside me.

Thank goodness for the music. It wasn't contemporary worship, and there was no band—only an old lady playing the organ. But they were old-timey songs that I kind of like, even though they talk about walking the wide road to destruction and blood running down the cross and other happy topics. You can sing four-part harmony to them, so Gillian and I took the tenor and alto parts. And with the amazed looks Callum was giving us, I felt happier than I had all morning.

"How do you guys know how to do that?" Callum whispered to me. "Sing like that, I mean."

"Years of practice," I whispered back.

"But you just met her at school, didn't you?"

"Sure, but we've known these songs since we were kids." I may have made a personal choice three years ago, but Mom had made her choice about how to bring us up long before that. "Besides, if you read music, you can sight-read the harmonies."

Callum might be the heir to the Penoco fortune and a championship golfer, but it was clear that, for him, reading music was on a par with learning Cyrillic.

It was also clear that I had gained enormous points with him by being able to do something he couldn't. I wasn't even very good at it, there being a huge difference between singing and carrying a tune. But points didn't matter to me. I just wanted him to think I was amazing.

Mission accomplished.

Now let's hope I didn't do something stupid to mess it up.

The house my dad had rented nestled in an oak grove on a hillside overlooking the bay, which was why the owner charged six grand a month. It didn't look expensive inside, though. Dad's not much for picking up after himself, which crazes my mother. Then again, she picks up the phone and calls a service to solve the problem and that's that. Anyway, it's on Lucas Valley Road, which was called that long before you-know-who moved in and built the Ranch, and was close for those late-night brainstorming sessions that are Dad's favorite part of the movie business.

My mother must have arrived just before us. She hadn't even changed yet. "Lissa!"

Oomph. I hugged her back, engulfed in a Monique Lhuillier suit and a cloud of Joy. Her shoulder blades felt sharp under the silk.

I pulled back. "Are the Babies of Somalia making you forget to eat?"

"Of course not. I'm eating. Like a horse." Which is what she always says. "Mind you, I'm not in the stable very much. I'm helping Angelina with the fundraising twenty-four-seven."

"Are their kids as cute as the pictures in *People*?"

"Way cuter. The youngest has me completely wrapped around her finger. You and Jolie are lucky you don't have a baby sister or brother at this rate."

It's hard to stay mad at my mom when you're actually with her. I did my best to hand my resentment over to God and turned to Gillian. "Mom, this is my roommate, Gillian Chang."

And my mom, being the way she is, hugged her instead of taking the hand Gillian offered.

"Did you name Lissa's sister after Angelina?" she asked, sounding a little winded.

Mom grinned and shook her head. "Not a chance. But she was the prettiest baby, and we'd just come back from a shoot in France so she could be born on U.S. soil, and *voilà*. There was nothing else to do but name her Jolie. Lissa was named for my Swedish grandmother, who was a pistol and whom I adored. And who is this?"

Mom turned to Callum, who barely had a chance to say his name before she hugged him, too. "I'm very happy to meet you two," she said, releasing him. "Come in. I have to get changed before we eat."

Dad stood when we came into the kitchen, and I flew into his hug. I talk about Jolie being a daddy's girl . . . well, she's not the only one.

"L-squared." (That stands for Lissa-love, in case you're thinking he's a bit weird. Well, he is, in that creative, not-quite-in-the-real-world way that makes you wonder how he and my mom ever got together.) I burrowed into the tweedy blazer with the shoulder pulling out of one side that he'd picked up in Yorkshire before I was born, and breathed in the smell of wood chips and lemon and smoke. He'd obviously had a fire in the fireplace last night.

"They treating you all right up there?" He looked me over as if checking for signs of manacles, or starvation at least.

"Yes. The food is good."

"Teachers okay?"

"Except for Bio. Genetics is nasty."

"But highly applicable in the real world."

"And Phys. Ed. is mandatory. Yuck."

"It's good for you. You can't lie around beckoning to the servants all the time."

"Dad!"

"No servants here, I'm afraid, except Mrs. Harris, who feeds me, and Bruno. So. When are you going to introduce me?"

I turned and ran through the introductions again. Callum looked as if he were staring into a klieg light—or the kind you see when you're approaching heaven.

"I'm a big admirer of your work, sir." He shook Dad's hand. "It's an honor."

Dad flushed. It really gets to him when people do this, and it happens all the time. You should have seen him on stage with the Oscar. He was a wreck.

"Thanks," he mumbled.

"I learn something from every movie, but *Malahat* was my favorite."

Dad stopped looking uncomfortable and began to look interested. Either Callum was sincere, or he'd done a massive amount of preparation. I preferred to think it was the first.

"That was Dad's labor of love," I whispered to Gillian. "It came out the year after I was born. Cannes loved it, but it totally tanked at the box office and Dad nearly had to go to work for Grandpa."

Mom came back into the kitchen, barefoot and in jeans and a crisp white shirt. "Mrs. Harris has lunch ready for us." She herded us into the dining room and watched as Callum pulled out my chair and seated me.

Wow. I thought they only did that in the movies.

Mom and Dad exchanged a glance but for once in their lives said the right thing: not one word.

Mom glanced at me over the spinach quiche, spring greens salad, and slabs of thick French toast. Then her gaze moved to my right. "Callum, would you say grace, please?"

Callum looked at her blankly. "Sorry?"

"Do you want to say grace?"

"Uh—" His eyes held appeal as they found mine.

"I'll say it," Gillian said, and did.

Mom raised her head and unfolded her napkin when Gillian finished. "I didn't mean to embarrass you, Callum. I shouldn't have made an assumption like that. I'm sorry."

My spine turned to jelly, and I slid down a little in my chair. I did not want to get started on religion. I wanted to talk about things that would make him think about me long after today. Could there be an earthquake now, please?

"You guys are Christians, right?" he asked.

"Not all of us," my dad said.

I saw a flash of pain in Mom's eyes before she was able to slip her company face back on. "That's right. Pass the French toast to Gillian, Lissa."

"I think I'm an Episcopalian." Callum managed to sound thoughtful, as if he were making a personal discovery while he wolfed down quiche. "We used to go to church when my grandma on my dad's side was alive, but she died when I was seven."

"And you haven't been since?" Dad asked.

I gave him a what's-it-to-you look, but it seemed he was treating the situation without his usual cynical humor.

"No." Callum piled French toast on his plate and poured a river of blueberry sauce over it. "Life got busy and I never thought about it much."

"You and I are outnumbered three to two, here, my friend," Dad informed him. "I suggest you change the subject while you can."

At the "my friend," a lazy grin lit Callum's face, and it was all I could do not to sigh and stare.

Take that, Vanessa. You may have known him since kindergarten, but I know what he wants out of life. And I can help him get it.

DLavigne	Is it official?
VTalbot	He had lunch with her parents. How official do you want to get?
DLavigne	He actually went? To church and everything?
VTalbot	Praise the Lord.
DLavigne	Sounds like you need serious retail therapy.
VTalbot	::eyeroll:: Like it matters.
DLavigne	I bet it does. You've liked him since freshman year.

VTalbot   Ancient history. You going downstairs? The new *Prison Break* DVDs released today. We can do three epis a night all week.

DLavigne   Save me a seat and a drool towel.

chapter 13

A S I SHOOK raisins and chopped apple into my oatmeal Monday morning in the dining room, Dani sidled up to me in line, cutting out the sophomore beside me. On my other side, Carly Aragon looked up and quickly glanced away, as if she didn't want to attract Dani's attention.

Smart girl.

"I've been hearing things about you." Dani selected a yogurt from the refrigerated case.

"Oh?"

"Is it true you hooked up with Callum yesterday?"

Did she mean hooked up as in "spent the day with" or hooked up as in "spent the night with"?

"Is that what people are saying?"

"I heard he went to church with you."

"That's true. And he met my folks. He and my dad really hit it off."

They'd spent nearly the whole afternoon yakking about storyboards and point of view and production values while Gillian and Mom and I hung out in the garden and talked about Angelina and school and, for some reason, how many different kinds of silk there are.

Not that I minded that Dad had essentially kidnapped my guy. Nothing wrong with my guy liking my family, either.

"So it's true, then. You guys are an item," Dani persisted.

"You'd have to ask him."

"I did. He wouldn't tell me."

I remembered what he'd said on our way to the field house. "Then I guess he wants to keep his private life private."

She looked at me like I was nuts. "What private life? We're his friends."

"Maybe he wants to have one."

I picked up my tray and left her standing there, not a lot wiser than she'd been before.

The truth was, I didn't know the answer myself. Spending a day sort of together and hooking pinkies did not a relationship make. And when Bruno dropped us off in front of Spencer yesterday, Callum gave me a big smile, said thanks, and loped off up the street, heading home. No "let's have dinner," no "want to hang out?" Nothing.

Were we together or not? Two hundred inquiring minds wanted to know.

"Hey."

Across our table, Carly's mouth dropped open as Callum pulled out a chair and sat down on my right.

"Hey," I said, the epitome of cool even though my heart had practically come off its moorings in my chest. "Yesterday didn't make you implode, I see."

"Not a bit." He started chowing down on his oatmeal as if he actually liked it. Didn't he eat at home before he left for school? "I had a great time."

"So did I. I hope it wasn't too much. Meeting the parents and getting grilled by my mom and all. I don't usually inflict that on guys I'm—" I stopped.

He glanced at me. "Guys you're . . . ?"

He'd saved my life. He'd met my parents. *Come on, Lissa. Just say it.*

"Not dating."

He nodded, started in on his toast. "My phone is gonna burn out its chips with people asking me about that."

I didn't know whether to apologize or not.

"I guess someone has to give everyone something to talk about." Awkward. Maybe humor would work. "May as well be us. As a public service."

"Or we could just prove them all right."

A piece of apple lodged in my throat, and I went into a coughing fit.

"Lissa, here." Carly grabbed my orange juice and tried to get me to drink it while Callum patted my back.

When I finally had myself under control, I croaked, "What do you mean, prove them right?"

I told you what that grin does to me. The effect does not wear off with frequent use, either.

"I like you," he said. "I noticed you when you were late to Bio that first day. You're not like the—" I thought he'd say *other girls,* but instead he said, "—people I've known all my life."

"I bet you say that to all the girls."

"Not true. You're different. Maybe it's the Christian thing. And even there you're not what I expected."

"What did you expect?" That I'd be like Gillian, all passionate about my faith and ready to shout it from the comm system?

He shrugged. "I don't know. Vanessa said—" He stopped, and I got the distinct feeling I didn't want to know what Vanessa said.

"I like you, too," I murmured. Okay, so not the most romantic place for this. All around us, plates clattered and kids shouted and talked, and somebody's CD player blasted the Gorillaz. But that didn't stop the warm glow that started in my cheeks and went all the way through to my heart.

"Want to do something tonight?" he asked. "The girls are going to TouTou's for dinner."

The girls. Gee, which ones would those be?

"Do you like it there?"

A lift of those broad shoulders, covered in the blue Spencer pullover. "It's okay. One of those places where it's all about the presentation. Which means you get a flake of salmon with a single chive laid across it for fifty bucks."

I had to smile. You should hear Mom on that subject. "I'm all over a good pizza, myself."

"Yeah, me too. Too bad Dining Services gives pizza a bad name."

"There must be a decent thin crust in this town somewhere."

He glanced at me, those willow-green eyes crinkling at the corners. "I say we go find it. Meet you out front at six?"

"I'll be there."

I hardly noticed Carly get up or heard her say good-bye. I was too busy basking in the glow of Callum McCloud asking me out in front of the entire dining room.

jolie.mansfield	Mom's freaking. Tell me about the new man!
LMansfield	Freaking how?
jolie.mansfield	In a good way. I hear he's a dish.
LMansfield	If you like them tall, green-eyed, and gorgeous.
jolie.mansfield	Same guy you were talking about before? Callum?
LMansfield	That's him. He's so nice. The most popular guy in school. We're going out tonight.
jolie.mansfield	Mom says he went to church w/you but he's not a believer?
LMansfield	Yet.
jolie.mansfield	Careful, L. You're not out to save him, are you?

LMansfield	Of course not. But maybe...
jolie.mansfield	Don't get caught in that trap. You concentrate on you and let God take care of him.
LMansfield	Duh.
jolie.mansfield	I'm serious.
jolie.mansfield	Lissa?

Despite my sister's tendency to give lectures nobody wants to listen to, the glow lasted until U.S. History, when we got a pop quiz that I totally wasn't prepared for. However, it wasn't like it would mess up my entire year's grade, so I refused to worry about it.

I had happier things to think about.

I got out of English at four and headed down the hall to the dorm. I wasn't sure two hours were going to be enough time to get ready.

A smaller hallway branched off to the left, and from down there I heard someone playing piano with such amazing skill I just had to see who it was. One of the teachers, maybe, who, due to some life tragedy, had had to leave a career on the concert stages of Europe to come here and teach rich kids the Beatles' greatest hits?

I peeked into the practice studio and blinked.

Gillian?

And suddenly I recognized the piece: Chopin's *Nocturne in D Minor*, a fiendishly difficult bit of work that you had to be a prodigy to master. And why did I know this? Because Mom is on the Youth Symphony Festival committee in Santa Barbara, and Natasha Paremski played it at a gala. She was a couple of years older than me, but it doesn't take a music critic to know a huge talent when you see it.

Gillian's talent was like that. She grinned at me over the baby grand's raised lid, and sailed into the finale. When she dropped her hands to her lap, I couldn't help it. I clapped.

"Thanks," she said. "That thing kills me."

"Why do you torture yourself with it, then?"

"Because it's what got me the scholarship. I figure I'd better keep it tuned up in case they wonder if they made a mistake and ask me to do it again. How do they know it was me on the CD and not some guy I hired from the New York Philharmonic?"

"They didn't make a mistake. You're brilliant."

"And you're making waves around here. I got a text from Carly that Callum asked you out, right in front of her and everybody."

"It's true. We're going to go find a pizza tonight instead of hanging out with Vanessa's crowd."

"Careful." She began running scales up and down the keyboard. The notes sounded like the patter of rain. "I might actually start liking that guy."

I laughed. "Gotta go get ready. Later."

In the end I decided to keep things simple. My eco-friendly Del Forte jeans, a T-shirt with a limited-edition Hannah Stouffer print, and my old faithful Roxy hoodie that I'd bought to celebrate graduating from gremmie to semi-competent on my surfboard. This is not something you decide. The other surfers let you know, and it was a big day for me. My definition of "big day" has changed, but I still wear the hoodie.

Achieving the social level I'd been used to in Santa Barbara was not easy, but after tonight, I'd bet a month's worth of makeup that I'd be in.

At ten past six, just when I was fingering my iPhone and wondering if a text nudge was in order, Callum pulled up in a black Prius.

"I don't know why I thought we'd be taking transit," I said as I buckled myself in.

"Normally I do. Around here, parking is a b"—he glanced at me—"bear. But if we're going for pizza, it'd take a while to get to North Beach on transit."

"Better you than me." The only sound we made rolling down the drive was the crunch of gravel under the tires. "I've had my license for a while, but there's no way I'm driving on these hills."

I'd no sooner said so than the ground dropped out from under us and we plunged down a street so vertical I thought for sure the rear tires would let go and we'd slide to the bottom on the hood.

But Callum just grinned and spun the wheel to take us to the left and down another hill. (He did realize this meant we were going to have to come back up all of them, right?) And, thank You, Jesus, ten minutes later we purred into North Beach and parked.

Lucky thing my jeans concealed my trembling knees as I got out and we walked around the corner to a hole-in-the-wall called Nonna Perla's.

"How'd you find this?" I asked as the waitress seated us and handed me a plastic card with the menu printed on it.

"Asked Brett. His dad owns a bunch of stuff in this neighborhood. Perla was his dad's grandmother. They come here a lot."

Talk about being connected. I'd have to tell Mom so she could file it in the mental PDA of restaurants she knows all over the planet.

It didn't take long for me to discover we had completely different taste in pizza, so I ordered artichoke hearts with pine nuts, basil, and feta while he went the traditional route and mainlined grease— pepperoni, bacon, and olives. Urgh. Barflex. Okay, so no one said the guy had to be perfect. Even Kaz can't resist pepperoni, despite the fact that he knows it makes him break out.

Kaz would love Nonna Perla's.

And why on earth was I thinking about Kaz when the most gorgeous guy in school—probably in the whole city—was sitting opposite me?

Our pizzas came—one perfectly baked, ten-inch yumfest for each of us—and Callum glanced at me.

"You want to say grace or anything?"

Awkward.

Of course I should. But I needed to tread lightly after my mom put him on the spot yesterday. "No biggie," I said. "I don't say it at every meal. Or at school."

Gillian does, my conscience pointed out. *Coward.*

Grace is a moment between you and God, I argued back. *It's not a political statement.*

The cheese was so hot, I burned my tongue. After gulping Diet Coke, I approached my dinner more cautiously. It was a shame the pain kind of drowned out the flavor, though. Callum wolfed his down and gave my plate a beady eye. "Not hungry?"

Truth? Not really. I was keyed up, and my brain jumped every which way after things to talk about. The last thing I wanted was to sit there like a lump, stuffing my face without a single interesting thing to say.

"A little of this goes a long way," I said. "It's the best pizza I've ever had."

"They do a good job." He helped himself to my last quarter. "Brett and I have been buds since middle school. We used to come down here to Little Italy after school and scam free appies off the relatives. We were growing boys. Couldn't make it until supper."

"Sounds like fun. So you were a foodie from childhood?"

"Nah, just hungry all the time. I was five-ten in seventh grade, and six feet by the time I was a sophomore. Mom couldn't keep enough food in the house for me. Besides, it was fun. Brett had a different sob story for every relative. The weirder they were, the more sympathy we got."

"I'm sure everyone knew what you were up to."

"Probably. What about you? What did you do when you were a kid?"

"Well . . ." I pushed my empty plate away, and the waitress whisked it off and refilled my Coke. "I stole a camel in Egypt once."

He snorted a laugh into his glass. "A camel?"

"I was seven. I didn't know you had to rent them from the guide. I just untied him, he knelt down, and off we went. I could hear the owner screaming at me in Arabic for, like, a block, before I figured out I'd done something wrong."

"Funny, you don't look like a felon." He grinned at me in a way that made me grin back.

"Yeah? What do I look like?"

"Beautiful," he said.

chapter 14

LOVE IS PATIENT. Love is kind. Love is not realizing you're about to fall off a San Francisco hill because all you can think about is the guy holding your hand.

Somehow he managed to drive one-handed back to Spencer and park under one of the pepper trees in front of the main doors. Despite the lights from the windows and the tall cast-iron lamps on either side of the stairs, all I could see of his eyes were hollows filled with shadow.

There was nothing wrong with my view of his mouth, however.

Would he?

Would I?

You bet I would.

"Can I kiss you good night?" he whispered, turning toward me and resting his right hand on the top of my seat.

I undid my seatbelt and tossed it over one shoulder like a woman throwing her inhibitions to the wind. "I don't know—can you?" I said wickedly.

"Come here and you can tell me."

I leaned a little over the center console and tilted my head.

He smelled of clean cotton and warm skin and a faint trace of cologne. Talk about a dream come true. Bottle that scent for late-night fantasies, girls.

My eyes slid closed as his mouth found mine. Oh, that mouth. It came through on everything his grin had been promising for days. Soft yet firm, and nothing hesitant about it. I'm no newbie in the kissing department, but a first kiss usually asks my permission. Waits. Backs off before I'm ready.

Not this one. Somehow he knew what to do to make my toes curl for real, to make my blood speed up in my veins, and to send my body temperature rocketing up.

By the end of that kiss, I was a watery puddle with steam rising off it, let me tell you.

And I was the one to break it. The female body needs oxygen, after all.

"Wow," I said when I'd dragged in a few breaths.

"Don't leave yet," was all he said, and I dove in for round two.

A surge of feeling deep inside me told me that even though we were sitting in the front driveway and someone could walk up at any moment, this was going to get away from me if I didn't grab my sanity.

I pulled back, my lips leaving his like the last farewell of Romeo and Juliet.

"Callum. Whoa."

He looked over my shoulder, and that blazing focus on me slowly faded to something approaching normality. "Sorry. Guess I got a little carried away."

"Do you hear me complaining?" I gave him a peck on the cheek. "Thank you for the pizza. And for tonight. See you in Math."

"Yeah. One more?"

"No way." I opened my door and scooped up my Marc Jacobs slouchy bag. "My temperature's already off the chart."

I heard him laughing as I slammed the door, and the Prius rolled away silently into the dark.

When I slipped into our room, Gillian looked up from the welter of books and papers spread around her on the bed. Her Mac notebook stood open in front of her, and as I closed the door, she paused the music on her iPod and pulled her earphones out.

"You look like you got something more than pizza."

I grinned at her. How could she see that from across the room? I resisted the temptation to do a quick check in the mirror. Way beyond obvious.

"We had a good time," I said at last.

"Where'd you go?"

"Someplace called Nonna Perla's in Little Italy. Brett Loyola's family owns it."

Gillian closed one of her textbooks. *Elements of the Chemical World.* Ugh. "He's the tall, dark-haired guy that hangs around with Callum, right? The one who's not Todd?"

I nodded.

"Carly has a thing for him."

"Carly Aragon?" Now, there was a hopeless situation. "How do you know?"

"He's in Chem with us. Every time he walks by, she loses it. Drops things. You know. And if she can find a way to bring him something or pass him a paper first, she does." She shook her head. "Yup. Definitely a thing."

"So who do you have a thing for?" I was in the mood to spread the joy. "Seen any prospects yet?"

"If I were looking for someone, it sure wouldn't be in that crowd. Not unless I were some kind of masochist and into unrequited love."

An instant replay of that kiss swept through my body in a tingly wave. "It doesn't have to be unrequited."

A sardonic glance. "Yeah, well, most of us aren't blond and

beautiful with movie directors for dads, okay? We have to be realistic."

"What's that supposed to mean?"

"Nothing. I hear there's a wicked genetics assignment for Bio. Did you get it?"

"What genetics assignment?" Was this the hot topic among the science geeks? Not that I was in the mood to care at the moment.

"I guess not, then." She slid off the bed and handed me a note. "Here. Some guy named Kaz called for you."

Three hours before, right about when we'd arrived at Nonna Perla's. Thank goodness he hadn't called my cell. "Did you tell him I was out?"

"Well, yeah."

"Did you say who with?"

With her back to me, she shut down her computer. "I didn't give out personal details. I said you weren't here, and I didn't know when you'd be back. We talked a bit, and he said to give him a call or IM."

How come I didn't want her to tell Kaz that I'd been out with Callum? Kaz was one of my best friends. He was always razzing me about the guys I liked, and then turning around and giving me a shoulder to cry on when it didn't work out, or telling me I'd done the right thing when it was me doing the dumping. I'd never kept secrets from Kaz. In fact, since he was as tight as a clam anyway, he was the perfect friend.

He was cute, too, if you liked the dark-eyed, sensitive skater-boy look. Some girls did. I preferred a more polished, upscale type when it came to going out, but Kaz was fun to hang with. His vocabulary sometimes scared me, but if you didn't mind looking things up in Wikipedia after a conversation with him, he was fun to talk to as well.

Okay, enough about Kaz. "I'll call him tomorrow."

All I wanted to do was crawl into bed and relive that kiss over and over. Imagine Callum smiling at me over his Coke and pizza. Hear the sound of his voice in my memory saying "Beautiful" until it echoed.

And then slide into sleep with his face in my mind and his voice in my ears so I could dream about him.

Because in dreams you never have to tell a boy to stop.

....

✉

To:	lmansfield@spenceracad.edu
From:	kazg@hotmail.com
Date:	September 30, 2008
Re:	Bite!

Hey L, I called last night but your roomie said you were out. Hot date?

I got some exciting news. DayStar Comix wants to look at the proposal for DEMON BATTLE.

!!!!!!!!!

I'm freaking. The e-mail came this afternoon and I can't sit still, can't concentrate. Wish you were here to grab my ankles and bring me down to earth. This is too big not to share and I can't think of anyone else to share it with. Jon and Aaron are OK but they don't do the happy-dance thing you do.

This is definitely an all-time danceworthy moment. Call me.

xo Kaz

....

I didn't call Kaz until after class on Tuesday. Not because I didn't want to, but between his classes and mine, neither of us was free until then. And since cell phones were verboten in all indoor common areas at Spencer (like classrooms and the dining room), that pretty much X'd out any opportunities there.

"This is just so cool," I said when he told me in excruciating detail about the contents of the editor's e-mail and the proposal he planned. "Someday you're going to be as famous as—as Frank Peretti, and I'm going to say I knew you when."

"Don't say that," Kaz groaned. "You'll jinx me."

"I don't believe in jinxes. If it's God's will, it'll happen, and nothing will stop it."

"You're right." I could practically see him rake his free hand through his hair. No wonder it always looked shaggy. "It's only a proposal request, anyway. The editor could hate it and I'll be back to square one."

"He won't hate it. The plot's original, your drawing talent is obvious in every panel, and you're my best friend. Three reasons it can't fail."

"Number three being the most important one."

"Of course."

Even half a state away, I could still make him laugh. And he could still make me feel like my opinion was the most important thing he'd hear that day.

"So enough about me. Tell me about life in the big smog."

"The big fog, you mean. It's good. Biology is killing me, but I'm having fun."

"And you're slaying the guys, from what I hear."

What had Gillian said? "Sure I am. Where'd you hear that?"

"Your mom, your sister. That reminds me. Katie says that if you don't call her, she's going to either drive up there or implode."

Katie Fedorov had been my best girlfriend since junior high, but after the Aidan debacle, it had looked to me like she wanted to be Homecoming Princess way more than she wanted to be my friend. Which is why I hadn't spoken to or messaged her since I'd left Santa Barbara.

"She could e-mail me. She doesn't need to use you for her messenger boy."

"I volunteered. Tiana's being her usual self. Getting voted Homecoming Queen hasn't done anything to improve world peace, lemme tell you."

Okay, so I'm only human. I could have told Katie that I was a nicer friend than Tiana Montgomery would ever be, but sometimes actions speak louder than words.

"I believe it. Well, she knows my number. She can call anytime she wants."

"Far be it from me to get in the middle of this," Kaz said. "Homecoming was a total snooze, but I got a slow dance out of it anyway."

"With Katie? Is there something there you're not telling me?"

He made a sound something like *chuh*. "I had one dance with her. There's nothing else to tell."

"Kaz Griffin. Katie? I can't believe it."

"Why not? A guy can only carry a torch for you for so long."

"Yeah, right. Hey, I need to go, okay? I've got this massively awful genetics assignment that's going to take me all week to finish."

"Call if you need help."

"No worries. My roomie's a genius. She'll give me a hand."

"That girl who answered the phone? Jilly something?"

"Gillian Chang. She's here on a music scholarship, but she's a science geek. I'd hate her if she weren't so nice."

And if I didn't know what a big heart she had. A big mouth, too, but a shot of honesty now and again wasn't a bad thing.

In most cases.

"She's nice, yeah. We talked for a while."

"Oh?" From what Gillian had said, the conversation was four sentences long. This was interesting.

"Yeah. She said you'd hooked the most popular guy in school or something. Congratulations."

"She has a big mouth."

"Hey, it's me. I'm not some random crank caller."

"She doesn't know that."

"Oh, I introduced myself. And it's not like you were going to get around to dishing the news. Or were you?"

"There isn't any news to dish. We went for pizza. No big deal."

"Uh-huh. I thought you said you had to go?"

"I do. 'Bye, Kaz. Good luck with the proposal."

"Thanks." Was it the phone connection, or had his voice deepened a little? "Take care of yourself. They didn't used to call it the Barbary Coast up there for nothing. I'm praying for ya."

He was such a sweetie—whatever the Barbary Coast had to do with it. "For you, too."

I hung up and glanced at the clock. Gillian was probably in the practice room. Just as well. I had to figure out how to ask her (diplomatically) to keep her editorial comments to herself. Kaz might be my best male friend, but geesh, he certainly didn't need to know all the details of my love life.

A girl had to retain some mystery.

Not to mention, the less he knew, the less I'd have to feel guilty about.

chapter 15

OKAY, LET ME rephrase what I had said about feeling guilty.

It's not that I planned to keep things from Kaz, or that I was going to do things I'd be ashamed of later. It's just that it felt a little weird to talk to a guy about another guy, that's all. I mean, Kaz has known me since I wore braces and thought Fendi was something that went on a car. We know each other's faults and flops. We mope together about the bad things (his parents splitting up) and celebrate the good things (the editor's request).

Callum certainly qualifies as a good thing on my side, but still . . . it feels weird, you know? Because under our friendship, under the razzing and the mutual admiration society we have going, I think Kaz likes me. As in, not a brotherly way.

So because he's my friend, I'm not going to tell him stuff that might hurt his feelings.

As I headed back to my dorm room before lunch, I passed one of Gillian's pink signs on the bulletin board outside the common room on our floor. That's right, it was Tuesday, so we'd be attempting another prayer circle tonight. Had it really been a week since that first disaster? So much had changed, and was about to change some more. I could feel it in the air, or, more accurately, in the glances people gave me in the hallways. People who hadn't given me the time of day during my first week had invited me to sit with them at breakfast today. Vanessa's outer circle—not the triad of terror, but the people who orbited around them—smiled at me. One girl, this gorgeous African-American called Shani, even offered to be my study partner for the genetics module.

Rumors of my relationship with Callum were clearly not being exaggerated.

Gillian looked up when I came in. "Hey. You're in Honors English, right?"

"Uh-huh." I let my tote go and it hit the floor next to my bed with a thud. "That sound is the essay I have to do on freeing the feminine in Kate Chopin's short stories."

She made a face at the poundage in my poor tote. "Chemistry is so much easier." She waved at her textbook, which to me looked as thick as a stack of pancakes. Then she held up an assignment sheet. "I have to write an Italian sonnet for Harryman in something called iambic pentameter, and I don't even know what that is. Plus I don't speak Italian. Duh. What is she thinking?"

"An Italian sonnet is a form, not a language." I grabbed my hairbrush. "I'll help you with it if you run me and Shani Hanna through Genetics for Dummies before Friday, when this project is due. Gahh. It makes my brain hurt."

"Deal," Gillian said happily. Someone knocked on the door. "Come in," she called.

Vanessa Talbot stepped in, and out of the corner of my eye, I saw Gillian's face go slack with shock before she turned away to pull her Mac out of her bag.

"Hey," I said.

"Hi, Lissa."

Okay, now I knew I'd reached a new social level. She'd remembered my name.

"I was hoping I'd catch you," she went on. "This can't wait until after class."

"What's up?"

"You probably already know this, but I'm the chair of the Benefactors' Day charity ball."

I nodded. Old news.

"The day is the big kickoff event to Spencer's year, so we want to make it perfect. It sets the tone for the whole year, you know? And does so much good for the community. So the committee and I have been working on it since, like, August, but now we're getting down to the wire and we need more people to help."

I nodded again. Made sense.

"So I'd like to invite you to be on the committee with us." She smiled in a way that told me I was not only moving up the social ladder at lightspeed—I'd reached the top. "We can really use your contacts in the movie world, and plus everyone agrees on how nice you are and what a good addition you'd make."

"Everyone?" Gillian asked from where she sat on her bed, checking e-mail.

"Everyone who matters." Vanessa looked her over and turned back to me. "So, anyway, we're meeting tonight to brainstorm possibilities for a special guest to do the welcome and lead the first dance. Whoever it is gets a nice big contribution to their favorite charity, so we get lots of coverage from their press people. A win-win, right?"

"Sounds like it," I said. "What time?"

"Seven thirty. In the staff lounge."

"The staff lounge? How are you going to get in there?"

"Since it's a school event, they let the committee meet there. It's quiet, nobody bursts in that you don't want to see, and you can spread out. Plus, Dining Services makes sure there's always food for the staff after a hard day's work." She grinned. "So, are you in?"

"Don't you already have plans?" Gillian asked me, sounding a little absent as she scanned her mail.

For a second I couldn't think what she meant. Visions of Callum and dresses and ballrooms danced in my head—again. Man, those really messed me up. Then I remembered.

"Oh." Prayer circle. "But that's at seven. We'll be done by seven thirty, won't we?"

"I suppose, if not too many people come and we pray at top speed."

Was she being sarcastic? Knowing Gillian, the answer was probably yes.

"Oh, that's right, you meet on Tuesdays, don't you?" Vanessa said. "Sorry, but I won't be there."

"That's too bad." Gillian didn't even look up.

"What about you?" Vanessa smiled at me. "Can we count on you?"

"Of course," I said. "Seven thirty. See you then."

When the door closed behind her, I glanced at my roomie, who hadn't taken her gaze off her screen. "That was nice of her."

She raised one eyebrow and finally looked at me. "You're kidding, right? You heard her. She doesn't want you, she wants what you can do for her."

"So? When my mom puts one of her committees together, the same principle applies."

"Yeah, but she's probably up-front about it. She doesn't have to tell them how nice they are and how everyone likes them before they'll do something for her. She gives them credit for a little self-respect."

"How do you know what my mother does?" I'd worked on a

few of her committees, and the fact that Gillian was right was not helping. But I certainly wasn't going to tell her so.

"I don't. I'm just saying."

"Sometimes you say a little too much. Did it ever occur to you that maybe I want to help? That it might be fun?"

"Did it ever occur to you that the only fun those girls get is from making other people miserable?"

"That's not true." Not entirely. "The whole committee is working for a good cause. I'll get community service credits. We need twenty hours every term, you know."

Gillian sighed. "Missing the point."

Don't care. "Are you coming to lunch?"

She shook her head. "I'll get something later. Are you coming to prayer circle?"

"I said I would, and I will."

"For half an hour."

"Gillian, I'll stay for as long as I can. What do you want from me, anyway?"

"Nothing."

Yeah, right. "It isn't nothing. Otherwise you wouldn't be sitting there looking like that."

With a sigh, she pushed her notebook aside. "I just think you should put your prayer life ahead of your popularity, that's all."

"There's nothing wrong with my prayer life." Okay, so last night I'd been so wrapped up in my evening with Callum that I'd completely forgotten about thanking God for it. But I'd make up for it. I would.

Besides, how could the Lord not know how thankful I was?

"My prayer life is a completely different thing from coming to prayer circle. That's a—an event."

"So what's Carly or some other kid going to think when you cut out halfway through to go do something else?"

"They'll think I went to do something else. They won't overanalyze it like you are."

"Uh-huh."

"What, you think I'm making some kind of statement about where God lands on my priority list? That's stretching it, Gillian."

She'd gone back to reading her mail. She sure must have a lot of it. "Whatever."

Look on the bright side, I thought as I stalked downstairs to get lunch by myself. *At least she didn't say that stuff in front of Vanessa.*

I'd never have lived it down.

IN ROOM 216, the thing with the pins in its eyes had been replaced with a clay map of Middle Earth. Everything else was the same, with the exception of Vanessa and the rest of them, who, as promised, had not shown up.

At ten past seven, Gillian gave me a casual glance that didn't fool me one bit. "Think Callum will show?"

"He's not one of those people who does the passive-aggressive control thing by being late. If he was going to come, he'd be here. We should get started. I only have twenty minutes."

The door opened and I couldn't help it—I sucked in a breath and my heart rate spiked, until Carly stepped in, along with Shani and the sophomore who had been stalking Gillian the other day at lunch, plus a tall, thin kid I vaguely remembered hanging out in the Physics lab. He closed the door behind them all.

"Am I late?" Carly asked.

Gillian shook her head, and I tried to look as if nothing had happened. "No. You're all just in time. And very welcome."

She introduced us to the newbies, and the tall guy turned out to be Lucas Hayes. No wonder I'd seen him in the lab. He was rumored to be competing in the Physics Olympics or something.

Yeeks. Geeks. The things they did for fun.

Then the door opened again and Callum stepped into the room.

Would I ever get to the point where he didn't take my breath away? I hoped not. Because seeing him was like Christmas morning, every time.

"Hey." His gaze held mine, like something out of a movie, and I couldn't look away.

"Hey. I'm glad you came." Not so romantic, but true.

He broke our connection and glanced at the others as if he'd just noticed them. "Actually, I came to get you." He smiled at me, then at Gillian.

"For the committee meeting?"

"Yeah."

"Wait a minute," Gillian objected. "It's only quarter past. We haven't even started."

"You guys go ahead." Callum held out his hand, and I took it as I spoke. "I'll catch up with you after."

And we were out the door. As we walked down the hall, I said, "Tell me Vanessa didn't send you. Are you on the committee?" He didn't strike me as the kind of guy you'd find on the phone, flushing free stuff out of corporations and hitting up the Junior League. He didn't strike me as the kind who'd let Vanessa use him as a messenger boy, either.

"Nope. I just wanted ten minutes alone with you."

Before I could recover, he swung me into an empty classroom. I had enough time to take a breath before his arms went around me and his mouth came down on mine.

W.

O.

W.

I wound my arms around his neck and kissed him back, hanging on like a drowning woman as I fell into the dark behind my closed eyelids. I lost vision, hearing, speech . . . everything except that kiss.

Finally Callum pulled back a little and rested his forehead on mine. He was breathing like he'd just run a mile, too.

"Wow," he said. I smiled, although he couldn't see it in the dark. "I should get you to where you're going." He sounded as if he didn't mean it very much.

"Do you have to?"

"No, but Vanessa's pretty serious about her committee. I don't want to lose body parts."

I chuckled. "How'd you know where to find me?"

He opened the door, and we stepped out of our bubble of sensation and feeling and back into the real world of paneled hallways and donor plaques.

"I called your room from the common room. When I didn't get an answer, I saw one of those signs and remembered it was Tuesday."

"Maybe next week you can go with me."

"Maybe," he said easily, loping down the stairs. "Here's the staff lounge."

He held the door for me and gave me a quick, intimate grin, standing so close it was practically a kiss. Then he closed the door behind me, leaving me alone with Vanessa and her committee. The good part was, everyone had seen that grin and the intimacy, so I went into that room with "Callum's girlfriend" written all over me.

While Dani and Emily exchanged open-mouthed glances and the other girls looked from me to Vanessa to each other, Vanessa frowned and took charge as if nothing had happened.

"Hi, Lissa. You already know Dani and Emily, so let me introduce you to everyone else." She pointed to four girls in turn. "This is Tessa Runyon, Todd's sister, who's a senior. Christina Powell and DeLayne Geary are both in our class. And this is Ashley Polk. She's a sophomore, but we're not holding that against her because her uncle's on the board at Neiman-Marcus." She smiled at Ashley, a petite brunette with the kind of big blue eyes you usually see on porcelain dolls. "Everyone, this is Lissa Mansfield. She transferred here from . . . ?"

"Santa Barbara," I finished. "Nice to meet you all." Good thing she hadn't asked me anything complicated. My mind and body were still half in the land of shooting stars.

Vanessa led me over to the table, where a glossy blueprint of the assembly hall was spread out. Little cutouts of tables, shrubs, and a bunch of squares and rectangles represented everything that would turn it into a ballroom.

With Callum, it would transform into something magical. But at the moment, the plans looked very prosaic. I squinted at a large rectangle. Was that supposed to be the stage?

I soon found out, since Vanessa was in charge of decorations and seating. Tessa was managing the music (live, of course, and did I think swing was passé, because if not, she could call in a favor and get Lavay Smith). Christina and Ashley's job was food and beverages ("We have three wineries desperate to donate— why can't we just use all of them?"), and DeLayne was running publicity and media relations.

"You and DeLayne are going to be working together," Vanessa told me, "because you'll need to tie in the staff of whomever we get for our celebrity host. Have you come up with any ideas?"

Uh, no. I'd had more important things to think about lately. I thought fast. "My mom is working with Angelina right now on a thing for the Somali babies. Why don't I see if she's available?"

So casual, Lissa. As if you have a lineup of A-list stars on your friends list that you can call whenever you need one.

"Perfect," Vanessa said, her eyes lighting up. "You work on that. If she brings Brad, they'll lead off the first dance with us and our dates—and Curzon and her date, of course."

Can you imagine it? Callum and me leading off a charity ball, whirling in the spotlight with Brad and Angelina?

Life just couldn't get better than that.

LMansfield	Mom, need to talk asap. Call me?
Patricia_Sutter	What's up? You OK?
LMansfield	V. OK. Need to talk charity business.
Patricia_Sutter	Tomorrow after supper. I'll be back at the house by then.

chapter 16

OUR PHONE RANG at ten to eight Wednesday night, and I dived for it.

"Hi, it's Mom."

"Hey. Busy week?"

"The usual. I swear, putting one of these things together is like herding chickens. Everyone wants to go in a different direction. I'm just glad Angie knows what she wants. Eventually everyone will fall into line, but in the meantime . . ." I could hear her blow a breath up through her blunt-cut bangs. "So. What's up with you?"

"More of the same, really. I'm on the Benefactors' Day committee and my job is to get a celebrity to kick off the event, give a speech, and lead off the first dance."

"Good luck with that one."

"It's not all work for the person. It's a fundraiser, and a chunk of the take will go to the celebrity's pet charity. So of course I thought of you and Angelina."

A couple of beats passed. "You want me to ask Angie if she can fly up to San Francisco to do this gig at your school?"

"It would be great, Mom. If I can get someone like her to do it, I will be so in."

"Aha. So this is about social standing, is it, and not about charity at all?"

"Of course it's about charity." I hated it when she took the high road. It always made me feel like I was standing on some other track, covered in everyone else's dust. "You don't know what it's like here. They're expecting me to come up with someone fabulous. And you know all kinds of fabulous people."

"What about George?" Mom asked. "Your father could talk to him. And it doesn't have to be an actor, does it? What about an athlete? The Giants and the 'Niners do charity appearances all the time."

"Mom." Was she kidding? Spencer was not about athletics. How could I explain this? "If I were putting together something for the Getty Foundation, I'd ask people like that. Old people relate to them. Angelina is different. She's young, she's cool, and she honestly cares about those Somali babies. She'd be perfect. Don't forget about the contribution. It could tie right into what you're doing for her."

Ooh, brilliant point. Surely she could see that.

"How big a contribution?"

"I don't know, but I can find out and text it to you tomorrow."

My mother sighed. "It's a lot to ask, especially when I'm catching her between films as it is."

"Please? Just mention it. That's all. If she's interested, great. If not, then I'll go to Daddy."

"You'd better go to Daddy and line up someone else anyway. This isn't going to happen, especially with only a few days' notice."

"It's almost two weeks."

"And her calendar works a year in advance. Take my advice. Call your father."

"But you'll ask her anyway?"

"Yes, I'll ask her. But I already know the answer."

"Thanks, Mom. I really appreciate this."

"Just search your heart, sweetie. Make sure your motivations are right."

A perfect moment under the spotlight with Callum? Securing my spot at the top of the ladder? What was wrong with working for that? Both my parents had always told me to go for my passion. That's exactly what I was doing. Obeying my parents.

"I will. Bye."

"Good night, darling."

Thank goodness Gillian was down at the library, looking for sample Italian sonnets we could use for a crash course on the form. Otherwise, she'd have been down my throat again about the committee. And not just that. Landing Angelina for the celebrity speaker was probably so outrageously out of her universe that I'd no doubt get an earful about pride going before a fall or overshooting my limits or whatever.

What Gillian needed was a little imagination and some chutzpah. Both of which I had in spades. Biology and genetics modules were one thing. Anybody could figure those out with the right study skills. Angelina was quite another—and getting her would need my particular set of skills.

To be on the safe side, though, I sat at my desk again and flipped into e-mail.

....

✉

To: GabeMan@atcom.net
From: lmansfield@spenceracad.edu
Date: October 1, 2008
Re: Celebrity speaker

Hi Dad. Remember that Benefactors' Day ball on 10/11 I told you about? Well, I'm on the planning committee and my job is to find a celebrity speaker to kick the event off and lead the first dance.

Any ideas? George? A ball player? Some hot boy actor running around begging for an audition? Time is short to nonexistent and I need help.

Thanks! Love ya.

Lissa xo

....

....

✉

To: lmansfield@spenceracad.edu
From: GabeMan@atcom.net
Date: October 1, 2008
Re: Re: Celebrity speaker

This thing is 10/11? Argh, I knew that. Don't ask much, do you? Let me check around. I'm assuming you asked your mother already. She has more people in her PDA than I've ever even met.

Love ya 2X.

Dad

....

When my iPhone chimed a couple minutes later, I expected it to be Dad calling back already with a brilliant solution to my problem.

But it wasn't.

"Callum," I said, in what I hoped was a warm, welcoming voice.

"Hey. Whatcha doing?"

"Working on committee stuff and waiting for Gillian to come back from the library. I'm helping her with her English homework."

"I miss you."

Warm tingles tiptoed through my veins. "Already?" We'd eaten lunch together. This was very good.

"Yeah. Why don't you ditch her and meet me in the common room? They're watching *Prison Break*."

"Uh . . ." If we'd been talking *Firefly,* that'd be a no-brainer. But *Prison Break*? Even for Callum, that was a stretch.

"We don't have to watch it. I staked out one of the couches in the back, next to the fire."

Oh. Now we were talking. But at the same time . . .

"Callum, I can't. I promised Gillian I'd do this so she'd help me out on this stupid genetics project. If I ditch her, I'm on my own."

"I'll help you with it. Eventually. After . . . you know . . ."

Oh my. I could feel my body temperature spike just thinking about it.

"Shut up. I hope you're alone."

"Brett's downstairs. I'm in his room. Sure you don't want to come? I'll only hold that seat for so long."

Part of me said, *He's trying to make you jealous* while the other part said, *It's working.* And another, saner part said, *You're not the kind who ditches her friends.*

But come on. Life was not all about work. *Prison Break* or not, I'd get to cuddle with Callum on the couch. Right there in front of everyone. He wasn't like Aidan, who'd convinced me to keep our relationship quiet so that it would be something precious and secret. Ha. So Tiana wouldn't find out, more like. I should be grateful that Callum was so fearless about us. So proud to have me beside him.

And I wanted to be there.

"Okay," I said. "Give me ten minutes to finish some notes and I'll meet you downstairs."

"That's my girl," he said, and disconnected.

That was me. Callum's girl.

And proud of it.

Gillian still hadn't come back, so I scribbled some notes, with little boxes meant to look like an Italian sonnet's structure, and left them sticking out of the right chapter in her English anthology. A quick touchup on my hair and a dash of lip gloss, and I was out the door.

When we got to the common room, the party had already started. A DVD played on the big-screen TV, but hardly anyone paid attention to it, whether it was because they'd already seen the episode, or because the show was just an excuse for everyone to get together. It took about five seconds for me to see that a couple of bottles of what looked like rum were making their way toward everyone who was drinking Coke. Cartons of orange juice and plates of munchies sat on an antique Victorian sideboard, and behind that I saw the top of a bottle of vodka.

My vision of snuggling with Callum next to the fire and feeling like the Chosen One wavered a little, but didn't break. I was not going to worry about the potential dangers of the situation, or argue right and wrong with my conscience. I, after all, had not brought the stuff. I was going to have fun and enjoy the moment.

"Get you something to drink?" he asked me.

"Diet Coke. Neat," I added.

He grinned. "Yeah. Me, too. I don't know what idiot snuck the liquor in here. They have to know Milsom is on duty patrol this week."

He walked away before I could point out that the innocent would get lumped in with the guilty if we got busted, unless there was a guard posted at the door to give us an early warning.

Still feeling a little uneasy, I made my way over to the couch. As soon as they saw me, a couple of juniors—weren't they in my English class?—got up, smiled vaguely, and disappeared.

Callum handed me my drink and settled beside me, his arm

slipping around my shoulders as easily as if we'd been going out since freshman year. There was something hard under the pillow I was leaning on, but with Callum heating up my whole left side, who cared? It was a minor annoyance. Probably just the arm of the old Victorian-style couch.

"What did you do, threaten everyone with bodily harm if they stole our spot?"

He grinned, then knocked back half his can of Coke. "Nah. I asked politely."

Kids settled around us on the carpet and on ottomans, talking about everything from golf clubs to how much they hated the math homework to where they were going for the weekend. I felt like Eleanor of Aquitaine and her court of . . . well, if not love, then certainly social triumph. While Callum talked as easily with DeLayne Geary and her little flock of Pussycat Doll wannabes as he did with Todd Runyon and the guys on the golf team, I chipped in an opinion now and then and tried to be as nice to everyone as possible.

If I was going to be queen to Callum's obvious king, I wasn't going to be like Vanessa Talbot. She might be rich and beautiful, but people wanted her to like them because it could be dangerous if she didn't. I'd be different. People would want to hang out with me because I was nice to them, because I didn't exclude them. The whole school would love me, and at the Benefactors' Day ball, people would applaud as Callum and I took the floor and—

"Heads up!" somebody called from the door. "Milsom!"

From my comfy seat on the couch, I watched the whole room scramble to hide the bottles of booze. Good grief, didn't they have a contingency plan? I felt calm and amused, secure in the knowledge that my can of Coke didn't hold anything it wasn't supposed to, and neither did Callum's.

Someone yanked out a bunch of leather-bound books on the shelf over the fireplace and rolled the vodka in behind them.

The bottles of rum were stashed under the seat cushion of two easy chairs, and a student flopped on top of each. When Milsom walked in, half the room was absorbed in munching cold pizza and watching *Prison Break,* while the other half sat comfortably around Callum and me.

"Hey, Mr. Milsom," Todd said. He lounged sideways in one of the easy chairs, his legs draped over the arm. He looked way more comfortable than a guy should with a bottle of rum poking against his hip.

"Don't be a suckup, Runyon." Todd raised his eyebrows and looked hurt. "Are alcoholic beverages being imbibed here?"

Only Milsom would use a word like *imbibe*—or *precipitating,* or *dulcet*—in any context outside chemistry class. The guy was worse than Kaz.

Twenty people shook their heads. Todd looked astonished that the teacher would even think such a thing.

Milsom shook his head with an expression of regret that was as fake as Todd's. "Unfortunately, my years of experience tell me differently. Runyon, Stapleton, Miss Mansfield. Stand up, please. Miss Geary, please remove the books over the fireplace."

DeLayne's dusky skin went pale. Moving hesitantly, she did as she was told while the rest of us stood. Callum and I looked relaxed in comparison to Todd and Rory Stapleton as Mr. Milsom confiscated the bottles they'd been sitting on. He took the vodka from DeLayne and then narrowed his pitiless glare on me.

What was he looking at me for?

"Miss Mansfield, if you don't mind."

I stared at him. "Sir?"

"Your cushion, Miss Mansfield. Knock off the innocence, please. I've been policing this room since before you were born. It, and you, have no secrets."

Did I look as dumb as I felt? "I'm sorry, sir. I don't understand what you mean."

He sighed, and in the future I could see a whole senior year's worth of chemistry grades slide off his desk, right into the trash can. "The bottle, Miss Mansfield. Under the cushion. Hand it to me, please."

"But there's no bottle there. I was sitting right—"

"Miss Mansfield, don't compound the trouble you're in by arguing with me. Hand it over, please."

For Pete's sake. Shaking my head at the stupidity of someone who refused to believe a perfectly innocent person when there was a herd of guilty ones all around him, I turned and yanked the pillow off the arm of the couch.

And stared in horror.

"Thank you, Miss Mansfield." He pulled the bottle of Jack Daniel's from between the arm of the couch and the seat cushion.

Breathe. Take a breath. Speak. "But I didn't—"

"Runyon, Stapleton, Mansfield," Mr. Milsom said heavily. "Head-mistress's office, eight o'clock tomorrow. The rest of you, turn off the TV and clean up this mess. You have twenty minutes until lights-out at ten."

Clanking a little with the weight of his booty, he turned and walked to the door, his heavy tread clearly audible in a dead silent room.

The door closed behind him and I turned to Callum, feeling a little desperate.

"What does he—I didn't know—"

Vanessa handed an empty pizza box to the person closest to her and dusted her hands, an expression of distaste battling with concern as she looked at me across the room. "Milsom is such a jerk," she said. "I hope you guys don't get expelled. I need you on the committee, Lissa."

Expelled?

I'd never even had a detention in my whole life. How could I be expelled? I hadn't done anything.

Callum put his arm around my shoulders and squeezed me against his side. "It's okay, Lissa. First offenders never get expelled unless there's blood or fire. Don't worry about it."

Blood. Fire. Expelled.

Cradled in the warmth of Callum's arm, I suddenly found it very difficult to breathe.

DLavigne   Hear what happened last night?

DGeary   I was there. Much carousing. Expulsions to follow.

DLavigne   Woo hoo!

DLavigne   Is it true Little Miss Christian got plastered and cussed out Milsom?

DGeary   Don't believe everything you hear. All I can say is she didn't do Jack. LOL

DLavigne   I have it from a reliable source that she did. And her parents are coming today.

DGeary   What for?

DLavigne   To take her to rehab, of course!

DGeary   Harsh. Wonder if we'll get Angelina now?

chapter 17

THE HEADMISTRESS GAZED at us, but I couldn't tell if her expression meant disappointment or disgust. Maybe a combination of both. I hadn't seen a look like that on a woman's face since I'd broken my mother's Venetian millefiori bowl during a game of tag at my eighth birthday party.

Broken being the operative word.

Mr. Milsom stood with his head cocked to one side, pretending to read the spines of her research books in the floor-to-ceiling bookcase. On the sideboard behind her desk sat the four bottles in question.

Exhibits A through D, I presumed.

"Well," the headmistress said on a sigh, "I'd expect this from you, Mr. Runyon, and possibly you, Mr. Stapleton, since impulse control isn't one of your strengths." That piercing brown gaze moved to me, and I swallowed. "But you, Miss Mansfield. I have to admit that after all these years of administering this institution, not much surprises me. This morning, however, I am surprised. I'd pegged you differently."

The door behind me opened, and I choked as Callum slipped into the room just in time to hear.

"It wasn't her fault, ma'am," Callum said, his usual drawl sounding a little breathless, as if he'd taken the stairs two at a time. "She had no clue that bottle was under her seat. I put it there."

"Mr. McCloud, why aren't you in core class?" Her dry tone indicated she saw right through him.

"Lissa hasn't done anything wrong. I can't let her take the rap for something I did."

"He *was* sitting on the couch next to her," Milsom put in, examining a disintegrating edition of Spenser's *The Faerie Queene*. Like a chemistry instructor would care.

"Yes, but according to your report, Bartley, he wasn't the one concealing the bottle."

"I wasn't concealing it," I repeated like a robot. "I thought it was the arm of the couch."

"Regardless of your intentions, the fact remains that the three of you were concealing the presence of alcohol. Stapleton and Runyon, did you know it was there?"

The boys looked at each other, then at her. "Yes, ma'am."

"Thank you for your honesty, at least. If I could prove you'd brought it to the party, I'd expel you. But since I can't, and Mr. Milsom can't, I'm going to settle for detention. A month of helping the maintenance staff with groundskeeping, an hour per day, five days per week, starting this afternoon."

Todd and Rory gaped at her, their mouths drooping like the mask of tragedy.

"Yes, I thought you'd like that. Report to Joe Wrigley's office after classes. You're dismissed."

They pushed out the door, and before it even closed, I heard them complaining to each other in the hallway, completely put out about doing manual labor. Ha. They should try being a production assistant on one of my dad's sets.

"Mr. McCloud, your desire to see justice done is to be commended, but you're dismissed also."

"But—" Callum began.

"Thank you, Mr. McCloud."

He looked into my eyes and squeezed my hand. "It'll be okay," he whispered.

When the door closed behind him, I straightened my shoulders and faced my fate. "Are you going to expel me?"

Ms. Curzon blinked at me over the fashionably narrow rectangles of her blond tortoiseshell glasses. "Expel you? Of course not."

"Should I . . . report to Mr. Wrigley at four, too?" What was she going to do?

Please, Lord, don't let her do anything awful. I'm sorry I was so stupid. I need Your help.

"For someone who says she's innocent, you seem awfully eager to be punished." She took off her glasses and looked me over. Had I buttoned my shirt properly? Was my hem the right length? I fingered the fabric nervously.

Could I do anything right, ever again?

"I'm not," I said. "Eager to be punished, I mean. But if I have to be, I'd like to get it over with."

"How are you coming along with arrangements for the Benefactors' Day ball?"

I stared at her. And this had what to do with the case currently before the jury? "Ma'am?"

She glanced at Milsom. "That was a fairly straightforward question, wasn't it, Bartley? I didn't speak in Tagalog or anything, did I?"

"No, Natalie. Though you do tend to revert to Cornish dialect when you're upset."

Oh, ha ha. All I needed at that moment was a pantload of sarcasm.

My cheeks burning, I said, "The arrangements are going well. My mother works with one of Angelina's foundations. She's going to ask her today if she can be our celebrity host. If that doesn't work, my father will call in a favor. We have a couple of local possibilities that don't need airfare."

"Lovely. Angelina would be a coup. I bet we'd get a sellout crowd. Thank you, Miss Mansfield. Well done. You may go."

I tried to get my mouth working properly. "But aren't you going to—"

She waved a hand. "Yes, yes, if you insist. I'll put a note in your file and notify your parents. Off you go, now. Here's a slip for your core class instructor."

I took the slip and escaped before any more weirdness ensued. The boys got a month's detention and I got a pat on the back? If I'd known that would happen, I could have dropped Angelina's name at the beginning.

Relief bubbled through me like pure oxygen. *Thank You, Lord. No more parties for me around here. Yes, I make mistakes, but You know I only make them once.*

I'd rather party one-on-one with Callum, anyway. And how about that sweet I'm-sacrificing-myself-for-you gesture, huh? If I'd been the tiniest bit insecure about our relationship, it was totally gone now. What guy would voluntarily take the fall for a girl he didn't care about? A lot?

That knowledge was almost worth the risk of expulsion.

A glance at the clock told me core class was half over. It wouldn't do me much good to show up now. I had my slip. What I really needed to do was to go back to my room and decompress for a few minutes. I could guarantee that all the others were agog to know what had happened, but I wasn't ready to face them yet.

Or to concentrate on core class. Who cared about romantic writers of the nineteenth century when your boyfriend had just done the metaphorical equivalent of jumping into the ocean to save you—again?

Gillian looked up from the *San Francisco Chronicle*—known to some as the *Comical*—as I slipped into our room. It must be her free period. She took a hit off her caramel latte and dropped her gaze to the paper once more.

Okay, so I hadn't exactly been the world's best communicator when I'd finally crawled into bed last night. Who could be, with the threat of expulsion hanging over her head?

"Oh, look. Here's Vanessa on the society page. How novel."

I took a deep, steadying breath flavored with the soft scent of caramel. "Gillian, I'm sorry."

She turned the page before I got much more than a glimpse of a micro-short dress and a big smile. "What for?"

"For ditching you and your English homework. For going to a party and not inviting you. For cutting out on you during prayer circle." When she didn't answer, I sat on my bed. "I'm about the world's worst friend."

"After last night, I can't say I know you well enough to be friends."

Ouch. And that delivery—like she was commenting on a new species of dung beetle. Ouch squared.

"You know me well enough to know I'm really sorry."

At last she looked up, flipping her hair behind one ear. Hurt lay behind the defensive expression in her dark eyes. "Did you know that the Chinese phrase for 'sorry' is *dui bu chi?* It means 'I can't look you in the eye.'"

Ouch cubed. Because I was having a pretty hard time doing just that. "I'd say the Chinese know what they're talking about. Did you hear what happened?"

"The whole school heard. When I went to get breakfast—there's a bagel there, if you want it—I was informed that you'd been taken to the drunk tank along with Callum."

"Really?" I said faintly. Good grief. The rumor mill was out of control. The bagel lay on my desk, and there was even cream cheese on it. "Thanks for the food."

"I didn't see you in the dining room."

"I had to go to Ms. Curzon's office at eight, along with Todd Runyon and Rory Stapleton. They got a month's detention."

"And what did you get?"

I shook my head and took a bite of the bagel. "Nothing. She asked me how the plans for the ball were going. It was surreal. Like she didn't care whether I had a whole barrel of Jack Daniel's under that stupid pillow."

"Or she knows you didn't do anything wrong."

Man, that bagel tasted good. "Which means that everyone is making up their own story."

She shrugged. "What do you care what they say?"

"I don't. You know who else was there?"

"I heard Callum got sent up, too. I was waiting to hear what happened to him."

"That's just the thing. He didn't get sent up. He came voluntarily, and get this—he took the blame for me. He was ready to do groundskeeping along with Todd and Rory. For me."

"So he got detention, too?"

"Uh-uh. I think they figured out he was just being gallant."

"Or he really was guilty and was playing gallant so those guys wouldn't take it out on him later."

Cynical much?

I finished the bagel and got up to wash my hands. "How can you say that?" I said from the bathroom. "Of course he didn't put that stuff there. But he was willing to take the hit so I wouldn't have to. He really cares about me."

"I guess he must," she said, but her tone was so neutral, I couldn't tell if that was a positive or a negative in her book. She closed the paper and got up. "I gotta go. See you at lunch."

"I'll save you a seat if I get there first."

She was no sooner out the door than my iPhone made its happy sound. And, oh joy, it turned out to be a three-way.

"Lissa," my mom said from Los Angeles. "I just got the most disturbing call from your headmistress."

"Me, too," Dad chimed in from Marin.

Don't you just love technology? Stereo parents.

I glanced at the clock. Three minutes until my next class. "Mom, Dad, I have a class at nine forty-five. Can we do this after school?"

"I trust your ability to be concise," Mom said. "Explain. Now."

Concise. Okay. I told the story in twenty-five words or less, sticking to the facts and trying not to sound defensive even though I felt attacked on all sides.

Though maybe not on Gillian's side. Maybe she was right, and Ms. Curzon really had thought I was innocent. If the call to my parents wasn't to say I was an immoral troll who should be taken out of school immediately, then sticking to the facts was the best plan.

"Do you know who stashed that bottle there?" Dad asked.

"No. But even if I did, I wouldn't say anything."

"Of course not. That would be social suicide. But—"

"Gabriel, that's hardly the point," Mom interrupted. "Lissa, we don't need to say that you have to think things through and make better choices."

If they didn't need to say it, why say it? I sighed. "No, Mom. I already told the Lord that I only do dumb things once. I do learn. Eventually."

"Maybe this Callum boy isn't as hot as you thought?" Dad asked.

What did he mean? "He's totally hot," I said. "He went up to Curzon's office and took the blame for me. It didn't work, but at least he tried. That's amazing, if you ask me. He could have been expelled."

I wondered if he'd been sent up to Curzon's office before . . . or what kinds of notes had been made in his student file. Maybe none. Maybe a lot. Just how big a risk had he taken for me? Not that it mattered. A risk was a risk.

"I know you have to go to class," Mom said. "Please remember that we love you and we want to see you do well at Spencer. I sincerely don't want any more calls from Natalie Curzon."

"Okay." Then I remembered. "Mom, did you get a chance to talk to Angelina?"

"I mentioned it to her assistant. They'll get back to me."

"When? I need to get Dad on the case if she says no."

"When they get back to me," Mom said firmly. "Bye-bye, darling. Have a good day."

"Bye, Mom."

"Love ya, L-squared."

"You too, Daddy." I disconnected and dropped the phone into my tote. Then I glanced at the clock again with a sigh.

Not even ten o'clock in the morning.

Could I go back to bed now?

chapter 18

WHEN WE GOT out of Math, Callum stopped me just outside in the hall, smiling down into my eyes in a way that made the pandemonium all around us fade into background music.

"You doing anything tonight?"

I shook my head.

"Want to come over to my place?"

"Your house?" I asked, just to clarify he didn't mean the common room in the boys' dorm or something.

"Yeah. My mom has a committee meeting, my dad's in Houston, and my sisters"—he did a one-shoulder shrug—"are both away at college. We'll have the place to ourselves."

Even if I'd had plans, I'd have canceled them. But he didn't need to know that. I pulled my iPhone out and made a show of checking a schedule I knew by heart. It's easy to remember a lot of blank space. "No, nothing. I'd love to come."

That grin again, the one I adored. "Great. Meet you out front right after dinner."

Needless to say, I spent the rest of the day spacing on classes and planning what I'd wear. When Gillian got back to our room I was deep in strategizing, clothes all over my bed and the closet doors draped in blouses and skirts.

"Don't tell me." She dropped her backpack at the end of the bed and sat, staring at the chaos. "You're going out with Callum."

"Why did I ever think that leaving half my clothes at Dad's was a good idea?" I moaned. "Callum invited me over to his place and I don't have a single thing to wear."

"Will there be tuxes and pearls?"

"No. No one but him and me."

"That nixes everything with a skirt, then."

Ah. The process of elimination. I was such a wreck that Gillian's orderly mind was exactly what I needed.

"Are you going hiking or snowboarding?"

"No."

"Then put away the jeans and sweaters. The hoodie and the Aran cable-knit, too."

I did. This did not leave much in the middle of the bed.

"So, totally alone, huh?"

"I hope so." Oh, yummy thought.

"Then if you're really going to do this, wear the velvet skinny jeans and the ruffled silk tank top, and the crocheted cashmere wrap sweater over it."

What did she mean? Of course I was going to do this. I hugged the sweater to my chest. Soft, approachable. "You're a genius."

She rolled her eyes. "Tell that to Milsom. I think he has a deliberate hate on for me."

"After last night, it can't be worse than the hate he has on for me." I dropped my voice. "'Miss Mansfield, don't compound the trouble you're in.'" I stripped off my fake wool skirt and white shirt, and kicked off my socks.

"Compounds," Gillian said with a grin. "That's exactly the

trouble *I'm* in. He doesn't listen when I say we'd get better results if we used magnesium in the stupid experiment." Then she sobered. "Hey, speaking of stupid experiments, don't you have some genetics thing due soon? When am I supposed to help you with that?"

The velvet jeans felt so soft and cuddly. I imagined cozying up with Callum, and a tingle went through me.

"Don't worry about it. It's due tomorrow but I'll ask for an extension."

"You can do that?"

I stared at her. "Sure. You mean you've never gotten one for anything?"

"No. I just turn the stuff in when it's due."

I shook my head. "Girl, girl. You have to learn to play the game. I'll ask for Monday, and we can do the project over the weekend. No biggie."

"If you say so." She paused, watching me slip on ballet flats.

"What?" I looked at my feet. "Would heels be better?"

"Do you think you're doing the right thing, Lissa?"

I stared at her. "Asking for an extension?"

"No. Going to Callum's place. Being alone. You know."

Why was she asking me this now? "What do you mean, the right thing? You just helped me find the perfect outfit."

"Yeah, aiding and abetting. That's me." She rolled off the bed and began to clear up her clutter.

I didn't really care for the sound of that. "Going over to his place is not a crime."

She shrugged, her back to me. "It just seems like you're moving awfully fast, that's all."

"Gillian, relax. We're just going to watch a movie or listen to music or something. We never get a chance to just be together at school. Don't worry."

"Who's worried?" She shoved some papers into her backpack.

"Come on. I'm starving. I hope you don't spill anything on those pants."

So did I.

⁂

THANK GOODNESS I didn't. The crocheted cashmere wrap sweater was a good choice, I reflected as I stood on the steps waiting for Callum. It might be Indian summer in the daytime, but nights in San Francisco get cool. In the distance, the downtown traffic sounded like the roar of the ocean, and birds cheeped as they settled down in the branches of the pepper trees. The scent of freshly mown grass hung in the moist air, mixed with exhaust from the street.

Gravel crunched, and there was the Prius.

We could have walked, as it turned out. The McCloud mansion (and I mean that; it was a huge old Victorian with a tower, for Pete's sake) was only a couple of blocks away. We whispered down a short slope under the house, where it looked like the garage had been scooped out of the hillside, and parked.

"Welcome to the family dump." Callum took my hand and we climbed a flight of stairs, emerging in a kitchen that was smaller than the one in my mom's Beverly Hills house, but that had the same kind of sweeping, wildly expensive view from the French doors. In Mom's case, she could look to the left and see Johnny Depp's place, and beyond that, the Chateau Marmont.

Callum opened one of the doors and I stepped out onto the terrace, gazing into the deepening twilight. "See that place that looks like a big lace doily?" He pointed to a house a few doors down. "Meg Ryan and Dennis Quaid used to live there before they broke up."

That was a long time ago. I wanted to know about *his* house. We went back inside and he led me through the place. High ceilings. Ancient, dark furniture. Rooms filled with sepia photographs of corseted women and gloomy men.

"This place looks like a movie set," I breathed. It had probably survived the San Francisco earthquake in 1906. "Who's your props manager?"

Callum snorted. "That would be Grandma. My mom's mother." He pointed to a nearly life-sized picture hung between two windows. It showed a woman in a fifties-era satin evening gown and fur wrap. A fox's head hung down next to her cheek and she looked out at the world as though it were already wasting her time.

The kind of picture Hollywood starlets used to have done when they married really rich old guys. Creepy.

"C'mon. My suite's upstairs."

Two sets of upstairs. I bet his family was in good shape, rabbiting up and down three stories all day long. The scary interior dec stopped here. Callum had a wide loft all to himself, with huge windows that opened onto a balcony. A desk with a complete gaming setup, including a wide screen, sat in the top room of the tower.

His bedroom opened off the loft and had a balcony as well. And, yes, no matter what Gillian may have thought, I only stood in its doorway. The room was a mess, but he didn't apologize for it, the way I would have. He just took my hand again and led me back to the loft, where a couple of squashy couches formed a right angle facing a plasma TV on the wall. A square glass table held sodas, water, and a pitcher of iced tea, along with a bowl of chips and salsa and a plate of—

"Are those *petits fours*?" I asked, eyeing the plate of tiny cakes with their fanciful icing, glistening with potential calories in the lamplight.

Callum nodded. "My mom has two weaknesses: speeding and pastry. I told our housekeeper we'd be doing her a favor by eating them, so she brought them up."

I toasted him with one. "To the public good."

I couldn't remember a time when I'd ever been so happy and yet so full of nerves and anticipation all at once. Snuggling next to Callum on a comfortable couch, watching *American Idol* and hearing him laugh at me because he caught me singing along with one of the songs. Drinking iced tea, which I normally don't do because it dries out my mouth, and finding it flavored with ginger and peaches. Breathing in the scent of old wood and furniture polish and the clean, warm cotton shirt he wore.

Could it get better than this?

And then he kissed me.

It could.

It absolutely, definitely could.

Three stories and a couple hundred years of scary family solidity just fell away, dissolving in that kiss. My jitters and nerves dissolved, too, as the joy of being in his arms poured over them like warm syrup. Again I had the feeling that time had stopped and there was no one in the universe except him and me. It was like God had just created us and hadn't gotten around to the earth and stars yet.

Had it felt this way with Aidan? I didn't think so. He'd been like a practice boyfriend. Someone who'd taught me what I didn't want, so that by the time I saw Callum, I'd know what I *did* want.

With my face buried in Callum's neck, breathing in the warmth of his skin, I finally forgave Aidan for what he'd done to me. It had been a favor, really. Can you imagine if I'd been tied to Aidan when Callum had started showing he was into me? Talk about torture.

"Hey, girl," Callum murmured. "We've really got it going on."

I smiled against his skin and nodded. "I bet Milsom doesn't know anything about this kind of chemistry."

His chest shook in a silent laugh. "I wish you could stay the night."

Impossible, but nice to wish for. "Me, too."

He lifted his head. "Yeah?"

"Sure. I could sleep with my head on your shoulder and serve you eggs over easy in the morning."

"You'd have to fight Carmela for the kitchen."

I laughed, getting into the fantasy. "I'd beat her to it, because of course we wouldn't have had any sleep the night before."

"Serious?"

What was he looking at me like that for? Like he'd just gotten five out of six lottery numbers.

"Right, Callum. Totally serious." *Not.*

"Because I really want you to. We're, like, spontaneous combustion. It could be great."

"It could." In my dreams. Because dreaming about an idyllic morning after was just that—a dream. The reality was that (a) his mom would come home eventually, and (b) the Bible was pretty darn clear on what God thought about having sex when you weren't married.

Sometimes reality just stunk. Fantasies were so much more rewarding.

"How come you didn't bring your stuff?"

"Huh?" I kissed him under the ear, where his skin was baby soft and sensitive.

"Your stuff. Clothes for tomorrow and stuff."

Okay, weirdness setting in. "Callum. I'm not going to stay."

"But you just said—"

"I said I *wanted* to. And I do. But I can't."

"Why not? Afraid your roommate will tell on you?" He grinned and smoothed my hair away from my face.

"No. It wouldn't be right, that's all."

"Feels pretty right to me. Come on. Stay with me."

Whoa.

Breathe. In. Out.

"Callum, I can't. I made a promise"—to God—"to myself that I wouldn't until I got married." I touched his face. "You understand, right?" Christian or not, I could just fall into that fathomless gaze.

"You haven't . . . *done it* . . . yet?"

I shook my head.

"Wow," he breathed. "That takes guts."

"It does right now, let me tell you. Sometimes I feel like I'll explode when I'm with you."

"Likewise." He kissed me. "Well, there are ways around it."

"Around what?"

"We can still get what we want without breaking your promise."

"I don't think so."

That grin took on a wolfish edge that was really sexy, yet it made me nervous at the same time. "Come on, girl. You've been with other guys. Don't tell me they didn't show you the ropes."

"Two guys, to be exact. One in seventh grade and one in sophomore year."

"Well, okay, then. But it doesn't look like either of them made you very happy, or you'd be with them, not me."

"That pretty much sums it up." I snuggled into the crook of his arm and tucked my feet under me.

He nuzzled my ear. "You can make me feel really good. I can make you feel the same way. And no loss of anything you want to keep, guaranteed."

"You already do make me feel good," I said softly.

"I didn't mean that way. Let's go in my room and I'll show you."

Oh. *That* kind of good.

"Um." I swallowed carefully. "Maybe not tonight."

"Why not? You want to."

Did I ever. But there was that annoying list in Galatians 5 to consider—the one about the acts of the sinful nature. And guess what item number two is? With that in mind, I'd promised to stay pure. On the other hand, I hadn't promised not to let anyone make me feel good, ever.

"Come on, Lissa," he whispered. "You want to. I want to. We may not get to be alone again for days." He ran his tongue along the rim of my ear, and I shivered. "And I promise you'll love it."

"I—I need some time," I said on a rush of exhaled breath, fighting against the urge to give in. "We've only been going out for a week. We're not in any hurry, are we?"

"Only that I can hardly control myself when you're around. Like now."

He looked pretty controlled to me, but what did I know? There was a world of difference in experience, in confidence, in sheer desirability between him and Aidan.

"I don't know." My voice trailed away. *How to feel completely lame in one easy lesson.*

"Hey." He kissed me again. "Don't stress. We'll work up to it." That grin. Why did it have this effect on me? "It'll give us something to look forward to."

Oh, yeah. You could say that again.

The question was, just how far forward did I want to go?

chapter 19

GILLIAN RELEASED THE SHEET, and the wind bellied the sails. We picked up speed and glided out into the harbor channel like a gull catching the updraft and soaring out into the blue. Today's lesson was tacking, and I clutched the tiller and tried to remember what the points of sail and wind direction were so that we wouldn't hit something and hurt it beyond repair.

The beautiful thing about sailing, though, was the way it gave you perfect privacy. Out there on the water that Friday morning, with the wind blowing and seagulls screeching and the odd motorboat trolling past at the harbor speed limit, no one could hear what Gillian and I were talking about.

"He thought you were serious?" Gillian asked, ropes in both hands and her attention totally *not* on trimming the boat. "He thought you were going to sleep with him?"

"Yeah. But he doesn't now. I explained that I wasn't going to do that with anyone except the guy I marry, and he's okay with that." I glanced around, but since we'd left the dock first, we were way out ahead of the rest of the class. "He even said it took guts to stick with what I believed in."

"So we can assume that he isn't a virgin, right?"

Right. I didn't want to think about his past. Not when his present was all about me. "Uh, yeah. I guess you can't look the way he does and not have half the girls in the school throwing themselves at you."

"I don't know if I'd like that," she said, so low I could hardly hear her over the wind.

"He's not a Christian, Gillian. It's not fair to hold him to some kind of standard he doesn't even know about."

"I know, I know. Hey, this is where we're supposed to tack. Tell me when you're going to make the boom swing over."

I tried to focus on what I was doing, and when we'd safely changed directions, she picked up where we'd left off.

"I guess that's why I don't hang out with guys who don't believe. There's so much stuff you have to explain."

"I don't know about that." Was she judging me for going out with Callum? I thought she liked him. "Aidan, my boyfriend in Santa Barbara was supposedly a Christian and he was no different than the rest of the guys. I was always the one slowing things down."

One of the reasons he'd dumped me, as it happened. The big hypocrite.

"Tack." By now, the others were beginning to catch up to us. "Keep an eye on Vanessa and Dani." Gillian changed position on the gunwale. "I don't want to be the one in the ocean this time."

"The thing is," I said, "I don't want to lose him by going all prudie on him, either."

"If he dumps you because of that, good riddance."

"Sheesh, could you be any more harsh?"

"Who wants a guy who only wants you for sex?" she asked. "That would be selling yourself way short."

"He doesn't. We have fun together. We talk. He likes some of the same movies I do. And he's put himself in danger twice now, for me."

"How do you figure?"

I waved at the dock in the distance. "Last week, when I fell in the water, and in Curzon's office yesterday. He took big risks for me. That's proof that he likes me for *me*, not . . . anything else."

"But how far do you go, is the question."

"Exactly. He said—" I stopped. This was my roommate, my friend. But some things should be kept private, shouldn't they? On the other hand, I couldn't get an opinion from someone I was coming to trust if I couldn't share, now, could I?

"What?" Her eyes were hidden behind her sunglasses, but her head turned toward me.

"Cone of silence?"

"What kind of friend do you think I am? Come about and go back the other way."

She loosened the sheet, the boom swung, and we jibed into the wind to turn around. Hey, I was getting pretty good at this. Vanessa and Dani's boat was coming up on us fast, though, and I needed to say this quickly.

"He said there were lots of things we could do without me breaking my promise to God. I was kind of afraid he was about to give me a demonstration, so I left a little while after that."

"If he's okay about not having sex, then that's that. If the 'lots of things' are what I think he means, I don't think you want to go there."

"It's like he wants to have sex without having sex, you know? And what am I—"

"Hey, Lissa!" Vanessa and Dani had swooped up on us like a big old albatross and passed on the right, waving like it was a race. "Come by my room after," Vanessa called from where she sat at the tiller. "We need to talk."

"I haven't heard anything about Angelina," I called back.

"Not about that." She pointed down the channel, where Callum was marooned as he waited patiently for Emily to figure out points of sail. "There are things you should know."

"That sounds promising," Gillian muttered.

"See you then," I called. Vanessa waved again, then turned to concentrate on her tack.

I glanced at Gillian. "What?"

"I think she heard us."

I instant-replayed the last minute. "No way. They were moving too fast, and there was too much wind."

"Yeah, blowing your voice right to them."

"I don't think so. She's been friends with Callum since grade school. She probably wants to tell me about the time he kissed some girl in kindergarten."

"You'll be lucky if that's all it is. I don't trust her, even if she does think you're her new best friend."

By this time we were coming up on the dock, where we were supposed to change places and let the other person steer for the second half of the class. So I kept it short.

"I'm finally getting along with her. I'm not going to do anything to rock the boat. I'll be as nice as I know how until I have a reason to do otherwise. How come you're so negative all of a sudden?"

"Negative?" she repeated, her voice going up. The boat bumped the dock and we changed places, doing our best not to make the thing wobble and tip us both off balance. "I wouldn't call it negative. I'd call it real."

EOverton	She's a VIRGIN?????
VTalbot	Straight from CMcC. But we already knew that.
EOverton	He'll dump her, don't worry.
VTalbot	Who's worried?
VTalbot	I bet she learns a thing or two first though.
EOverton	Does he really like her?
VTalbot	Some people like milk and white bread too.

EOverton	Not if they have Godiva and Courvoisier.
VTalbot	You're sweet. And you spelled it right.
EOverton	It's sitting in front of me, that's why.

———

VTalbot	Your mom's a Christian right?
DGeary	You got it, baby. Glide Memorial all the way.
VTalbot	What's the deal?
VTalbot	With Christians I mean. What are they about?
DGeary	Believing in Jesus, like He's the Son of God.
VTalbot	I know that. I mean like life.
VTalbot	They don't have sex, right?
DGeary	How do you think I got here?
VTalbot	V. funny.
DGeary	Not before the wedding.
VTalbot	Ever?
DGeary	I guess some do. But they don't tell.
DGeary	Or they're nasty virgins.
VTalbot	?
DGeary	They do everything but.
VTalbot	Got it. Tx.
DGeary	You getting saved, girl?
VTalbot	Okay bye.

———

DLavigne	It'll never work. Even you can't be that convincing.
VTalbot	Watch and learn, girlfriend.
DLavigne	Tell all afterward.
VTalbot	Don't I always?

Vanessa's room was just like ours, minus the silk, instruments, and Johnny Depp posters and plus a flat screen, several huge pillows, and a massive wall mirror. What does that tell you?

She called, "Come in," at my knock and waved me onto a pillow, where I leaned against a bed.

"Drink?" She tossed me a soda from a mini fridge under the desk and wrapped her French terry dressing gown around herself.

"Thanks." I sipped, wondering what to say. "So, Vanessa, tell me about my boyfriend" seemed kind of abrupt. Not to mention weird.

She sat on the opposite bed and tucked cotton balls between her toes. "I've got a pedi scheduled Monday, but I couldn't stand this color another second." She'd already removed the offending shade and a bottle of Scarlet Seduction stood ready beside her foot. "Want to come with us later?"

"Where to?"

She shrugged. "I don't know. I don't feel like clubbing, so probably we'll just find a restaurant on Fillmore and have dessert, then maybe catch a movie at the vintage theater."

"That sounds fun."

She glanced at me slyly as she began painting her toes with the skill of a pro. "No date tonight?"

That pointed glance punctured the balloon of my self-confidence, even though I had a valid reason to be a wallflower on a Friday night.

"No," I said glumly. "Milsom practically gave me detention when I asked for an extension this morning. He said this stupid genetics project is due today, no exceptions, so I have to send it by midnight tonight or get a zero. He's even going to check the timestamp on the e-mail."

"Bummer."

"Total bummer. The good thing is that Gillian doesn't have plans, so Shani Hanna is coming over and they're both going to help me with it as soon as I get back."

"Lucky you, to have a brain for a roomie. I'm on my own in here, but I think Dani wants to move in with me." She sighed. "The only thing she's good for is an endless supply of Jelly Bellies."

"That's not a bad thing." I smiled. "I love Jelly Bellies."

"You're not watching your weight."

I wasn't sure if she was referring to herself or Dani. Both of them were size 4, not Amazons like me. Best not to go any further with that one.

"So," I said. "You wanted to talk to me about Callum?"

"Yeah." She ran a critical eye over her toes. "Do you think this red is right with my skin tone? Is it too dark?"

I leaned over to look. "No. I think it's pretty. What are you wearing with it?"

"My black True Religion jeans and new Manolo slides."

"It's perfect, then," I said. "You want something with authority to counter the black. If you went any lighter no one would notice."

"You're right." She smiled and started on the other foot, her wet hair as glossy and sleek as a wet seal. "You're good."

"Many years of experience."

"Yeah? Does Callum know that?"

O-o-kay. Not talking about nail polish anymore. "We told each other about our pasts." Well, I did. I'd have to follow up on his.

"And you're cool with it? That boy has really been around. Some girls would think that was intimidating." She glanced up. "You know. Competing with so many memories."

"I figured I wasn't exactly his first. And if he broke up with them, the memories can't be that good, right?"

With a laugh, she returned to her careful strokes. "That's a healthy attitude."

"Are you one of them?"

She shook her head and the light arced along the curve of her hair. "Nope. I'm practically the girl next door. Known him all my life. We made mud pies in his grandma's garden when we were three and have the scars to prove it. We had no idea she'd just planted some kind of priceless Asian tree there."

The image made me smile. "His grandma seems kind of scary."

"Did you meet her?"

"No. I don't think she was home. He said everyone was out."

"That sounds like him. He's a very private guy. Not exactly the type to bring a girl home to meet the family. Most of them don't last long enough to do that, anyway."

"I hope I'm different."

She glanced at me. "Oh, you are. Not his usual type at all."

"Oh? What's his type?"

I shouldn't have asked. I didn't want to talk about other girls: I wanted to talk about him. And here was someone who'd known him all her life, who could tell me fun little details that a guy would never say out loud.

"I did some asking around," she said. "About being a Christian and what they believe and stuff."

Did Vanessa never answer a direct question? Or did she just have massive ADD?

"You could've asked me. I've only been a believer for three years, but I know the basics."

"Like what? Leaving out the Jesus stuff."

It took me a second to get my jaw off the floor. "Um. It's all about the Jesus stuff."

She capped the bottle and considered her toes with a critical eye. Which was good, because I was still pretty off balance. Vanessa? Asking about being a Christian? I mean, the Lord works in mysterious ways, but this was right off the map. "Here be dragons," as Kaz would say.

"But what about the logistics?" she asked. "Like, when you hook up with someone like Callum, how do you handle it when he wants to get physical and your religion says you can't?"

"That's kind of personal, Vanessa." Plus, I hadn't figured that out myself yet.

"Okay, forget Callum. Just in general."

"Why do you want to know?"

She shrugged. "Well, if I ever want to go to church, I need to know the drill, don't I?"

I took a breath and tried to marshal my flapping thoughts into order. "There's more to it than whether a person has sex with their guy. There's belief and trust and faith, and showing love to people, and prayer. It's, like, a whole lifetime of giving back to God, because He came down here and died for us."

She frowned. "Okay, getting heavy."

"Sorry."

"We're getting off topic anyway. What if I wanted to have sex, but didn't actually do it?"

"Join the club."

"No, I mean, there are ways to keep your guy happy and still have limits. Technically, you'd still be . . . what's that word? *Pure.* I could do that, couldn't I?"

Why did she care? This had to be one of the weirdest conversations I'd ever had. "You know, you could just stay away from the situation altogether," I suggested. "The Bible says that God can deliver us from temptation, but sometimes it's just smarter not to go there, you know?"

"Yes, but if I was dating Callum, temptation would be walking around in front of me, looking totally doable, all the time."

"Isn't that the truth." I took a moment to appreciate the visual, even though I wasn't about to "do" anyone, including him. "I'm always going blonde around him. I'm sure I'm going to flunk Math and Biology because of it. Who can concentrate when even the back of his neck turns me on?"

She smiled, and it wasn't the nasty smile, or the patronizing one, or one I'd even seen before. It was genuine—the kind friends share. At least, it looked that way to me. Well, if God wanted me to talk about this stuff with Vanessa Talbot, who was I to argue?

"He's just as crazy about you." At my look of surprise, she

leaned back on her pillow. "We do talk, you know. Don't you have a guy friend you talk to about stuff?"

"Yeah, back in Santa Barbara." Maybe Kaz would have some insight into how guys thought. That he'd be willing to break ranks and pass on, anyway.

"Callum and I don't have any secrets. Besides the fact that I'm really good at finding them out"—she grinned—"I've known him too long. And the truth is, he loses interest fast. If you want to hang onto him, you need to know that."

Could that warm, intimate gaze that I'd drowned in last night cool to indifference? Could he be driving some other girl crazy next week instead of me?

Not if I could help it. "He's interested," I said firmly.

"He is now. What are you going to do to make sure he stays that way?"

"Fascinate him with my sparkling conversation?"

Her mouth widened in a smile. "You're really pretty, Lissa. I'm sure you won't have any trouble keeping him right where you want him."

"That means a lot to me," I said with complete honesty. "Coming from you. Being one of his oldest friends, I mean."

"I know I haven't always been as nice to you as I could. But when I needed help with the Benefactors' Day ball, there you were. I don't think I thanked you for that."

Wow. Did Vanessa Talbot just apologize to me?

"Don't thank me until Angelina actually walks in the door. We haven't got her commitment yet."

"We will. If Callum can't resist you, how can a Hollywood star?"

Laughing, I got up to go. "I really have to go do something about this genetics mess. Have fun tonight."

"We will. Thanks for coming by."

I took a breath, then the plunge. "If you ever want to talk about God or—or anything else—you know—I'm available."

Not so graceful, but the best I could do, considering that just a day or two ago, she was the dragon at the edge of the map.

But she only nodded and gave a little wave, and I headed back up to my room, where Shani, genetics, and Gillian waited.

Mysterious ways, for sure.

VTalbot	Gaaaahhh.
DLavigne	Wassup?
VTalbot	She PREACHED at me. I feel gicky, like someone poured syrup on me.
DLavigne	Told you.
VTalbot	She's thinking about it.
DLavigne	Losing the Big V?
VTalbot	I'm gonna win the bet.
DLavigne	You're so not. That Prada suede is MINE.
VTalbot	You watch. She totally believed I was thinking about being a Christian. And I gave her all kinds of good advice. Heh.
VTalbot	So. TouTou's? 8:00?
DLavigne	I'm there! Emily's on her way.

chapter 20

I DIDN'T WAKE UP until midmorning Saturday, which was pretty early considering the grueling hours of work last night. But thanks to Gillian, I got the wretched project in to Mr. Milson at eleven fifty-eight p.m. by the school's e-mail clock.

I fumbled for my glasses on the desk and scanned the room. No Gillian, but a banana and a muffin wrapped in plastic sat next to my mouse, holding down a piece of paper.

> Carly and I went to Starbucks on Fillmore.
> There 'til eleven, then taking train to Union Square for retail therapy.
> Coming?

I so did not deserve her.

The Starbucks was just around the corner, so if I showered fast, there'd be time for what I needed to do before I left.

Kaz answered his cell on the first ring.

"Liss! I was just thinking about you."

"GMTA. How are ya? What's the news from the editor?"

"They turned it down." Just like that, all the life leached out of his voice, and I could picture exactly what was happening as we talked. "I don't even think they read it. They just tied it to a boomerang and it came back."

"Have you been lying there moping?"

"I never mope."

With the same tone, I said, "Have you been lying there thinking misanthropic thoughts and contemplating the end of your career?"

"Yes, actually, now that you mention it."

I laughed. "Kaz Griffin, there are a zillion graphic novel publishers out there. Cross those guys off the list and send it to the next one."

"But I wanted *them* to publish it. Their production values are the best."

"God knows where He wants it. Keep trying and praying until you find out where that is."

"Yeah, yeah. Are you done being all perky?"

"We personal cheerleaders have to be perky. Expensive, too. You will be billed."

"I knew there had to be something in it for you."

"Well, now that you mention it . . ."

His tone changed again. "Uh-huh. What's up? It's that guy, isn't it?"

"Am I that transparent? I really did want to know what happened with the publisher."

"I know. Thanks. My dad thinks it's a waste of time. I was beginning to think so, too."

"Open the blinds. Let the sun in. That'll help."

"You got some kind of webcam, or what?"

"Yeah. In the A/C vent, behind the grille."

I heard him get up and open the blinds. "Okay, Psychic Girl, what's on your mind?"

Where to start? "I need to know how guys think," I blurted.

"Big topic. Need parameters."

"How they think about girls."

"In general? If you knew, you'd never like any of us again."

"In particular. Like, the girl they're dating."

"Depends on the girl, I guess."

"Not helping."

"Sorry. Well, if I liked your friend Gillian, say—"

"What?"

"Just as an example. She's smart, she uses words like *precipitate,* and she's beautiful."

"How do you know she's beautiful?" They'd only spoken on the phone once that I knew of. Where'd he get off making assumptions like that?

"Her pic's posted on her MySpace, dummy."

"Oh." Gillian had a site? "OT warning."

"Right. Well, as I was hypothetically saying, if she were my girl-friend, I'd want to be with her all the time. We'd do fun things together. We'd hang out and talk and listen to music. You know. Maybe I'd even teach her to surf, too."

"And Gillian, being the brilliant person she is, probably wouldn't ride over you with her board the first time she got up on a wave."

"Are you still embarrassed about that? It could have happened to anybody. And the swelling went down in a couple days. No biggie."

"What about sex?" I blurted.

"Ask your mother, not me."

"Kaz!"

"Oh, you mean with my hypothetical girlfriend? Nuh-uh. You know I don't believe in that."

"What if you did? What if you weren't a Christian?"

"Liss, what are you getting at? Just spit it out."

I sighed and tried to calm down. Next thing I knew I'd be

getting all weepy. "I've been going out with Callum almost two weeks." Eight days, but we were definitely into the second week. "It's wonderful and I'm crazy about him, but I'm afraid I won't be able to hang onto him."

"You? Doubt it."

Kaz was so sweet. "Thanks, but he has this rep of going through girls fast."

"You'll be different."

"That's what I'm hoping, but it's getting pretty intense pretty quick here."

"How intense?" His voice got quiet and very serious.

Uh-oh.

This was a dumb idea. I should never have called him. Our chemistry was private between me and Callum. That was what made it intense—duh.

"Liss, is he giving you pressure about going farther than you want to?"

"No-o-o," I said slowly, feeling my way around the fib. "But I'm hearing stuff. That he might expect me to."

"He's got the wrong girl, then, right? He knows about your commitment?"

"Yeah, I told him."

"Then that should be that. You've got nothing to worry about."

"Well, apparently there are ways you can keep a guy happy and interested without breaking your commitment."

Silence.

"Kaz?" Nothing. "Can you hear me now?"

"I heard you." He sounded kind of winded. "Stand by for reboot."

"Oh, come on. Don't go all wussy on me. We've talked about this stuff before."

"Not with you as the subject. It was always what-if."

"It's what-if now."

"Sounds more if-then to me."

"But have you ever done anything like that? Gone all the way without technically going all the way?"

"Uh, no."

"Have you thought about it? I mean, if you did it, would that make you love her more? Or less?"

Another silence. "You know, I can honestly say my imagination has failed me. And that takes some doing, as you know."

"Ka-a-z!" I wailed. "This is important."

"Liss, I don't know." I could just see him raking a hand through his shaggy brown hair and having it fall back into his eyes again the way it always did. "If you're thinking of doing stuff with this guy, I'm the wrong person to ask. You're not going to get permission from me."

"I don't want permission, I want your opinion! Who else am I going to ask?"

"Just a suggestion—Callum?"

"Thanks a lot."

"He's the one you're supposed to be talking with about your relationship, not me."

"I can't just ask him flat-out how far he wants to go."

"Why not?"

"Good grief," I said in exasperation. "How romantic is that?"

"How romantic is this whole situation? You're supposed to be thinking about dances and corsages, not how you can hang onto your purity and have sex at the same time."

The air rushed out of my lungs. Surprise and indignation and hurt rushed in.

I snapped my phone shut so hard I was sure I'd dislodged the processor. But I didn't care. I threw it at my tote and stormed into the bathroom, turning the water on as hot as I could stand it.

So much for my best friend. He could take his advice and shove it right up his oh-so-virtuous . . . exhaust pipe.

GILLIAN AND CARLY were standing outside Starbucks when
I got there.

"Hey!" I realized that this was the first time I'd ever seen Carly
Aragon smile, except for the time in the dining room when Brett
Loyola asked her to get him a Coke if she was getting up to get a
refill herself. That smile showed a pair of amazing cheekbones and
a big, deep dimple. She should do it more often.

"Do I have time to grab a caramel macchiato?" I asked. "I don't
want to hold up the show."

"Sure, no hurry," Gillian said. "We'll wait here."

The drink went a long way toward sweetening my temper. I
should never talk to people before I get my caffeine fix. Poor Kaz.
I'd send him an e-mail tonight and apologize for hanging up on
him.

What he'd said still rankled, though. I was *so* not trying to have
sex. How crude. What I was trying to do was understand the
male brain. Figure out what it might take to make Callum happy
without compromising my own beliefs. Why was that so bad? Why
did Kaz have to make it sound so awful?

By the time I got out on the street again, I was ready for major
retail therapy. "I'm so glad you guys thought of this," I said as we
walked to the BART station. "The search for the Benefactors' Day
ball gown starts now."

Gillian nodded. "May as well start at the top. Saks and Neiman-
Marcus are both at Union Square."

"So is Macy's," Carly put in.

"The stuff I like isn't at Macy's," I said.

"The stuff I can afford is," she replied quietly.

Oh. Okay. I'm not spoiled—really, I'm not—but it had been a
long time since I'd had to worry about what it said on a price tag.
The bills went to my mom and she paid them and that was that.

And the other students at Spencer Academy weren't the type to worry about price tags, either. We were talking trust fund babies, the offspring of corporate giants, and families with old money. But there was really no nice way to ask if she was a scholarship student, so I kept my mouth shut.

"No biggie," Gillian said. "Both of you are going to Chinatown, too."

"What for?" Carly asked. "We're looking for dresses, right?"

"Right. And the kind I want isn't in stuffy old Neiman-Marcus."

"You're getting your dress in Chinatown?" I needed to clarify. Surely she wasn't going to pull something off a hook outside a street vendor's display. Street chic was one thing, but you didn't take it literally. "Do you know a designer there or something?"

"No, but my aunt does."

"You have family here?" Carly looked almost envious. "I wish I did. Everyone I love is either in San Jose, Texas, or Mexico."

"My dad's sister lives on the Peninsula with her husband, my two cousins whom I haven't seen since they were eight, and her mother-in-law. My dad told them I was going to school here, and we've been talking over e-mail. She knows this great designer called Tori Wu and she's driving up to take us to her shop. We're supposed to meet her at three."

Since it was eleven fifteen now, that didn't leave much time to find a dress that would take Callum's—and everyone else's—breath away on the big night. But Rome wasn't built in a day, now, was it? This was just a fact-finding mission. I still had time.

"Why are we going to department stores, anyway?" Carly asked, a little diffidently. "We'll only wind up with clothes that everybody else has. We should go to the garment district."

"Which is where?" I'd been to the garment districts in L.A. and New York, and Carly had a point. Who wanted to turn up in a Chloe chiffon one-shoulder that two other girls had? Scooping everyone with a hot, as-yet-undiscovered designer could be fun. Especially since the samples on the racks were one-of-a-kind.

"Third and Brannan."

"And you know this because . . . ?"

"My sister went to the School of the Arts here. She took me one time when I came up for the weekend."

"I never knew you had a sister," Gillian said.

Carly shrugged. "She's a lot older than me. She's in Austin now, doing sound production for a recording studio."

Cool. The things we find out about people when we hang out with them.

The garment district in San Francisco looks like any off-downtown industrial neighborhood, with little studios tucked into upstairs lofts, and street-level shop fronts in between dry cleaners and parking garages. I had to hand it to Carly, though—she really had a nose. Like my mom in a Hungarian village, Carly could look at an inconspicuous doorway with a hand-lettered sign directing fabric deliveries around to the back, and somehow decide that we should drop into this or that one as opposed to some other one.

And when I saw her in the curtained-off space that passed for a dressing room, in a pale pink silk corset with a floating, transparent overskirt trimmed with miniature razor ruffles, I converted completely.

"Wow," Gillian breathed. "That's The One."

"It would look fatal on me. But you've got the body to carry it, Carly," I agreed.

Twisting to see the back, Carly made a face at us in the mirror. "Thanks a lot. The corset is squishing everything out the bottom. Don't you think it makes my butt look huge?"

"It does not. It looks sexy. And your waist looks microscopic."

"How much is it?" she whispered.

"Only seven hundred for both pieces," Gillian whispered back.

Carly's shoulders drooped, and she considered her reflection.

"Maybe if I just get the corset, I can put a skirt I already have with it."

"Don't you dare," I said before she talked herself into it. "The contrast between the corset and the skirt totally makes the whole outfit. It'll make a fabu entrance."

"It'll make Brett sit up and beg," Gillian put in slyly.

"Tell you what." She was weakening, I could see it, so I moved in for the clincher. "I'll buy the skirt and you can pay me back. Or not. I don't care about that. I just care about you looking beautiful at the ball."

She blinked rapidly, and her eyes got that glassy look mine do when I'm trying not to cry. "I can't do that, Lissa."

"Of course you can. Come on. Let me unlace you. We only have two hours left and I haven't found anything yet."

Designer corset: three hundred fifty dollars.

Micropleated chiffon skirt: four hundred dollars.

Making a friend so happy she cries: priceless.

We went on up the street, and even though she'd found what she needed, Carly's nose didn't take the rest of the day off. At the top of a third-floor walkup over a body shop, one of those weird coincidences happened that really makes you wonder.

The designer was a Hungarian girl named Maja Fortescu, who wasn't much older than my sister, and with my mom's nose for food still in my head, we got to talking while we looked over the rack. It turned out her older brother had got a bit part in the film Dad had shot in Budapest, and suddenly the designer was treating us like family.

She had someone brew us a pot of strong herbal tea, and went into the back. When she came back, my jaw dropped at the beauty between her hands.

"This dress brand new for winter." She shook it out and Gillian drew in a breath. "You try on."

I couldn't get stripped down fast enough, despite the fact that the place was so small, there was no dressing room at all, just a mirror and some good lights.

Maja dropped it over my head, made some adjustments to the underpinnings, and when I faced the mirror again, I had turned into a princess. Or at the very least, a member of visiting nobility. A silver chain helped to hold it up, halter-style. A straight column of fragile white silk, beaded in silver so that it rippled and glinted like water, fell from the top of the bodice. Underneath, I could feel hidden bones snugged against my ribs, but to anyone looking on, it would just seem to be floating on my skin.

"Wow, Lissa," Carly said. "You look like something out of a dream."

Maja grabbed a bunch of my hair and pulled it straight back. "You wear hair like this, sixties-style. Silver or diamond clip, or silver band. You have such?"

"My mom does." She could overnight my grandmother's Art Deco diamond clip to me. "I'll take it."

While Carly's outfit wouldn't make Mom flinch, the bill on this one would. But it was all for a good cause. If I was going to be among the committee members leading off the ball in front of Angelina, the trustees, and the media, then it was going to be in this dress.

"I'll make sure all the papers know the designer," I told Maja as I signed the credit slip. "Can I have your card? I bet my mom and her friends would be interested, too."

I was just full of good deeds today. Spreading the joy. After talking to Kaz, I could use a little joy, right? This field trip had been exactly what I needed. And it wasn't over yet.

We grabbed a burger at Lori's off Union Square and then headed into Chinatown to meet Gillian's aunt. Gillian checked her iPhone as we dodged the crowds on the sidewalk, weaving around displays of fans and silk pajamas and lace collars and T-shirts that said "I ♥ San Francisco." Grocery stores displayed their wares right on the sidewalk, with mountains of apples and kiwi fruit and baskets of dried things that I think were mushrooms. Tiers of chrysanthemums announced that there was a florist somewhere behind them, and old women presided over carts, cooking snacks that smelled heavenly.

"Did you grow up in a place like this?" I asked Gillian, charmed.

"Me? No." She looked a little surprised, then ducked to avoid a porcelain doll swinging from the corner of a stall. "We live in an apartment on the Upper East Side."

Oh. Rapid adjustment of preconceived notions.

"My aunt said to meet her at this corner." She looked from the map on her iPhone to the street sign. "I guess we're early."

The words were no sooner out of her mouth than a woman waiting at the light waved. "Gillian!" She looked both ways and dashed across, ignoring both the red light and the fact that she wore four-inch Jimmy Choos. Ooh. From the fall collection, too.

"Sweetie!" She swept Gillian into a hug. "*Zao!* I'm so happy to see you. Wow, you're as tall as me now. And so pretty. I bet your dad sleeps across the threshold with a rifle, huh?"

Gillian laughed and tried to stem the flow. "Aunt Isabel, these are my friends, Lissa Mansfield and Carly Aragon. My aunt, Isabel Chang-Zhuo."

Each of us got a hug flavored with some exotic perfume I'd never smelled before, but that seemed to lie on Isabel like really expensive lingerie.

"Well, you guys are a bonus," she said, beaming. Then she saw our bags. "You've found dresses already?"

I nodded. "Carly took us to the garment district and we totally cleaned up."

"Now it's Gillian's turn." She tucked Gillian's hand into the crook of her arm. "Come and meet my friend Tori."

Tori Wu's studio was the top floor of a warehouse a block over, with a dry cleaner and three souvenir shops on the bottom floor.

The designer herself was tiny, shorter than Gillian's five-two, but her talent was huge. I could see that as soon as we stepped into the airy space. She already had a couple of models on hand, as if we were getting a private showing.

Maybe it was for Isabel's benefit, maybe not. As I've said, I'm no artist, but I sure know how to appreciate genius in other people. And Tori Wu had it. Another name I'd recommend to my mom the moment I saw her.

The two women embraced, and Isabel introduced us. Another pot of tea appeared on a low table, accompanied by tiny, translucent china cups. We got comfortable and the models got to work.

There were only six dresses, but if I'd been Gillian, I'd never have been able to make up my mind.

"This is impossible," she moaned to us. "I want them all. Look at that lime green with the black beading. Doesn't that knock you out?"

Isabel leaned over. "Who do you want to be at this event, Gillian? Asian Goth? The ingénue? Sixties starlet? Go with a look and Tori can work with you to get the right fabric."

Gillian looked from me to Carly. "Well, these guys are doing the soft floaty look, so I should do something different. I really like that green and black, and the way everything flows out from the beading at the side of the waist. I even like the raggy edges."

"Asian Goth it is." She nodded at the model, who strolled over so we could get a closer look. "See? This is what holds it up." The model turned so Isabel could unzip the back and show us. "This is Tori's trademark. Construction becomes illusion."

"Short skirt or long?" Tori asked.

"Long," we all said together.

"I'll take your measurements, and you can try it on."

The model was taller than Gillian, and had fewer curves, but even so, the dress made us all sigh as Gillian pirouetted in front of the mirror.

"I'd go with a lighter green," Isabel said. "She's only sixteen, after all."

Tori nodded. "And we'll take off the sleeves. You have pretty shoulders. If I move this cap here"—she demonstrated with the shoulder seam—"it will show them off."

"No décolletage," Isabel said firmly. "She doesn't advertise what she's got."

"Of course. When is your event?"

"The eleventh," I said. A week away, and I still hadn't heard from Angelina. Gulp.

"I will have it ready by the tenth, and delivered."

"Thank you so much." Gillian tried not to crush the skirt as she hugged the designer, but Tori didn't seem to notice. She hugged her back as though Gillian were her daughter.

"That dress was meant for you," Tori said. "It makes me happy that you like it."

"Like it? I'm totally in love," Gillian gushed in a way I'd never seen. She was not the gushy type, but hey, sometimes good clothes will do that to you. Or maybe it's what the clothes represent—a beautiful face that you turn to the world, hoping someone will fall in love with you in return.

Or, I thought as we said good-bye, maybe I was just projecting.

LMansfield	Mom, can you send me Grandma's diamond clip for the 10/11 dance? I found the perfect dress.
Patricia_Sutter	Of course. Can't wait to see it.
LMansfield	Any word from A?
Patricia_Sutter	!! So sorry, Lissa. It's been insane. She said yes.
LMansfield	Wooooooohooooooo!
Patricia_Sutter	One hour. We fly her in, she opens, dances, leaves. Okay?
LMansfield	Perfect. Major donation coming. Ten percent of the take.

Patricia_Sutter	She has another engagement in L.A. that same evening so it will be tight, but doable.
Patricia_Sutter	And no B. Just A.
LMansfield	I'll take her any way I can. I owe you. Thanks so much!
Patricia_Sutter	Heard from your dad?
LMansfield	Not in a couple of days. Why?
Patricia_Sutter	No reason. I'll be home Wed night. Love you.
LMansfield	Love you 3X.

————

LMansfield	We got her! Angelina confirmed.
VTalbot	Coooool! Props to you!
VTalbot	Thought any more about what we talked about?
LMansfield	Yes. Been kinda busy dress shopping tho.
VTalbot	Ooh fun. Find anything?
LMansfield	Yes.
VTalbot	Just yes?
LMansfield	It's hard to show fireworks and ecstasy on IM.
VTalbot	☺ Committee meeting Tuesday. Let's talk after.
LMansfield	Any chance we can move to Monday? I have a commitment Tuesday.
VTalbot	Hm. Okay. Guess we shouldn't keep the good A. news to ourselves. Monday same time, same place.
LMansfield	Deal.

chapter 21

SUNDAY MORNING I planned to go to church with Gillian, so I was already up at eight thirty when the phone rang.

"Hey," Callum said, and at the sound of his voice, my insides melted.

"Hey. You're up early," I said in my best morning-after voice, even though we hadn't had a night before. Isabel had taken us to dinner after the shopping trip, and even though Callum had left a message on my iPhone, it was late when she dropped us off and I hadn't talked to him until now.

"I have a nine-thirty tee time with the old man. Want to come?"

An opportunity to meet his dad, balanced against the sheer boredom of being the audience to a golf game. So not fair. But it was kind of moot.

"I'm going to church with Gillian."

"Oh, right," he said easily. "What about after? Want to go to the beach?"

Did I! That took no balancing of pros and cons at all. "I'd love to. We'll be back by noon. Come and find me in the dining room, okay?"

"Will do. Wear a bikini."

He was laughing as he hung up, so I had no idea if he was serious or not. Probably not. The skies outside our window were clear and sunny, but the coolness in the air told me there was probably fog on the ocean side of the mountains, dropping the temp into the high fifties and making a bikini not just dumb, but possibly life-threatening.

I may stink at genetics and trig, but when it comes to beach weather, I know my stuff.

While Gillian showered, I signed onto e-mail to see if Kaz had replied to the apology I'd sent last night.

....

✉

To: lmansfield@spenceracad.edu
From: kazg@hotmail.com
Date: October 5, 2008
Re: Re: I'm sorry

You don't have to apologize, L. I was out of line talking to you like that. I'm upset, I guess. The guy has to be a lowlife to put you in a position like this. Making you question your decisions, I mean. Or yourself.

Okay, not coherent. Just sincere.

Or jealous.

Incoherent. Need coffee before church.

Love, Kaz

....

I stared at the screen. Jealous? Had he even proofed this before he'd sent it? In a pre-caffeine haze a guy could say anything and regret it later.

But it explained a lot.

Uh-oh.

Gillian emerged from the bathroom and I closed my e-mail. I was going to have to figure out how to handle this.

Thank goodness for church. Gillian had asked around and found one just one train stop from school, for those occasions when both my parents were out of town, and as we sang "Blessed Be Your Name," my problems just seemed to fall away. Or maybe they got reprioritized, I don't know. But as I listened to the pastor talk about the fruit of the Spirit, I realized that Kaz honestly cared about me, and instead of being something to "handle," I should just be glad I had him in my life. I might not like it when he told me the truth, but I needed to be grateful he did. Kaz saw me as I was and cared about me anyway.

After all, the first fruit of the Spirit is love, right?

AS WE'D AGREED, Callum came to find me in the dining room. Let me tell you, there was more than one envious pair of eyes on us as we walked out of there together, off to do something fun. I'll be honest and say it made me feel good, but what made me feel even better was the way Callum held my hand on the curvy drive over to the beach, only taking it away to shift gears. Sometimes he just took my hand with him, pressing my palm into the ball of the gear shift as he went from third to fourth on the straight stretches.

When we reached San Gregorio, I got out of the car and breathed in my favorite scent—kelp and wet rocks and spume from off the waves. The air was misty with it, and with fog. I'd been right about the weather, and my Aran cable-knit felt cozy and warm, especially since I'd layered under it with a T-shirt and my embroidered Roxy hoodie.

And—just in case—a bikini.

"Have you ever surfed?" I asked Callum as we followed the meandering carved track of a seasonal stream toward the water line.

"No, never. You?"

I nodded. "I love it. I haven't been doing it very long. Haven't traded out my longboard or anything, but it's so much fun." I scanned the sets as they rolled in. Half a dozen guys in black neoprene suits waited in the line. If I'd had my stuff, I'd have been out there with them. Three-foot waves and not much traffic? Perfect.

"Yeah?" Callum's easy smile bewitched me. Again. I keep saying that, don't I? But it was true. "Little Surfer Girl, huh?"

I glanced at him. "You listen to the Beach Boys? My mom has all their records in vinyl. She never has time to listen to them now, though, even if she did set up the turntable."

"Nah. My dad had a CD in this morning. Some kind of remix." He looked out at the waves, where the first guy in line had popped to his feet and taken off. "Doesn't look too hard. Kinda like skateboarding."

I made a mock-choking sound of disbelief in my throat. "Surfing isn't as easy as that guy makes it look. On a skateboard, you don't have to deal with an ocean that has a mind of its own, not to mention sandbars and rocks."

Another sidelong glance at me. "So when am I going to see you out there?"

"As soon as I get my board and suit from my dad's, if you want."

I could think of nothing I'd rather do than spend a day on the waves with Callum. We'd have to do it quickly, though. Indian summer couldn't last forever, and while I'd done it down south, I'd bet that winter surfing up here was a lot colder.

"Maybe after this Benefactors' Day gig, we can all rent the stuff and you can teach us."

My nice little vision lurched to a halt, as if someone had hit Pause on the remote. "Us?"

"Yeah. Make a day of it. We talked about this before—you, me, Vanessa, Brett, all you girls on the committee. The ones we hang out with."

"Oh. Sure we could, but I was thinking it could be just you and me the first time. It's easier to learn without an audience."

"Did I tell you Vanessa and Brett made it official?"

Whoa. Newsflash.

Poor Carly.

"Really?"

"They came for dinner last night, and you couldn't peel them off each other. I called to invite you, but you didn't pick up."

"Brett and Vanessa? I thought he was just friends with her, like you are."

"Yeah, so did I. But I guess Vanessa had a change of heart. And he's not going to say no."

That was a funny way to put it, but I didn't care. Vanessa was off the market, and my relationship with Callum had just become a couple degrees more secure. Especially since he'd invited me to do something with his family twice in one day. The fact that I couldn't go didn't change the fact that he'd wanted me to.

So the surf lesson wasn't going to be private. I could live with that. Everything else was perfect.

We didn't say much as we walked, hand in hand, for at least a mile down the beach. It was great to be with someone you could just be quiet with, you know? No pressure. No performance. Just an appreciation of the wind, and the skittering antics of the sandpipers, and the bright colors of pebbles worn to roundness.

At the same time, though, silence like that makes you think. And I was thinking about what Kaz had said about talking to

Callum about this sex thing. The farther we walked, and the more I got used to the feel of his hand around mine, the more I wondered if maybe Kaz was right. After all, this involved just two people. How come I was going to everyone else for advice instead of being honest with the one I cared about?

"Can I ask you something?" I said.

"Sure." He squeezed my hand and tugged me closer to the water line. The fog finally lifted enough for the sun to glow through a thin membrane of cloud, so I took that as a good sign.

"I've been wondering . . . I mean, I've heard that you've had a lot of girlfriends."

He glanced at me, puzzled yet smiling. "Yeah? You're the only one around right now."

I smiled back, both at the reassurance and at the way he accepted "girlfriend." "I know, but rumor has it you go through them pretty fast."

Now the smile lessened and the puzzled look increased. "Sometimes it doesn't work out. Are you worried?"

"No . . ." *Oh, just spit it out, Lissa.* Guys hate when girls beat around the bush. "But I wondered if this thing about making love would make a difference. Between us, I mean."

No smile, all puzzled. "What thing?"

"You know. Remember, I told you I'd made a commitment about not having sex before I was married?"

"Yeah. But I thought you said we could work around that."

"Well, that's the thing. What exactly does that mean?"

The smile had come back, at least. But I couldn't tell if it was a smiling-at-Lissa smile or plain old amusement at a silly question. A flush crept into my face.

"You want me to tell you about the birds and the bees?" he joked.

Okay, feeling small and very dumb. "No, I want you to tell me what you want from me."

"I don't want anything more than you want to give." Now, that was better. Something inside that had been coiled up with embarrassment began to relax. "When you're ready for it, I will be, too." He stopped walking and ran both hands up my arms. "You've gotta know that I want you. I want to spend the night—I told you that already. Does that answer your question?"

"Sort of," I mumbled. When had I ever thought I was even a little bit experienced? I should be handling this better. The girl was the one who said how far things went, right? Then how come I was doing the asking?

"What brought this on?"

I shrugged. "I was talking with a friend of mine and he said I should go to the source. So that's what I'm doing."

"He did, huh? Anybody I know?"

"No. An old friend from Santa Barbara."

"You're talking about me with old boyfriends?" His tone was so casual, as though it wasn't a big deal. That should have warned me right there.

"He was never a boyfriend. I've known him forever. He's the one who taught me to surf."

"So you're talking with him about our love life and he told you to ask me? Next time you talk to him, tell him I sure appreciate that."

Moments too late, it dawned on me that Callum could get upset. He'd picked up the pace and, worse, dropped my hand and jammed both of his into the pockets of his thick gray hoodie.

"What's the matter?" I demanded, slipping my hand under his arm to slow him down. "I didn't go into details. Mostly because there aren't any. I was just asking. I kept it general."

"It's hard to keep *that* general."

"Well, I did. Callum, stop. He doesn't know anything."

"How long will that last?" he wanted to know. "You talk to everybody."

"I do not." At this pace, we'd be back at the car in a few minutes.

"What about Vanessa?"

"She's your friend."

"And that Chinese girl?"

"Her name is Gillian. And she's my friend."

"Great. So you're gossiping about me to three people. So far. Who's next? The paparazzi?"

"No." My throat ached and the wind had whipped tears from my eyes. "I don't gossip. And I never, ever talk to the rags."

Finally, at the car, he looked me full in the face. "What do you call it, then? What we do is between us, Lissa. It's nobody else's business."

"I was just—"

He opened my door from his side and I fell into the passenger seat as if my legs could hardly hold me up.

"I hate people talking about me." He gunned the engine and backed out of the parking spot with barely a look at what might be behind him. "I hate them watching me. I hate that I can hardly walk home after school without a backup escape route. I told you before how I felt about it. It's hard enough with everybody else, but I thought with you at least I'd have someone to talk to that I could trust."

"You can trust me." I could hardly get the words out through my misery. "I didn't think talking to my friends and yours was so wrong."

"It's wrong for me. Yack yack, behind my back. It makes me sick."

Did he mean I made him sick, too? I didn't have the guts to ask. I wanted to cry, and at the same time, I didn't want him to see me do it. So I just stayed quiet, blinking back tears and trying to hold it together until we got back to San Francisco.

How could such a harmless thing as talking over my options

with my friends—and his—make him so mad? These were people he knew, not some reporter from the *Enquirer*. How could you not talk over something as important as your commitment to God versus your commitment to your guy? How did a person figure these things out otherwise? Ask their parents? Look it up online?

I talked over most things with Mom and Dad, but their time was scarce and getting them focused on my stuff was harder than you'd think. Other than when they got calls from the headmistress, of course. That focused them pretty quick.

As we climbed the last hill that would take us to the Spencer drive, I reached a calm enough place that I could speak without crying.

"Thanks for taking me to the beach."

No reply. He stared straight ahead, gripping the wheel as though we were in an F-18 and about to fly through those gates on one wingtip. I gulped. Was this how a relationship ended? With one mistake and cold silence?

I picked up my stuff from the floor and pushed my door open as the car rolled to a stop. "I guess I'll see you in class tomorrow."

He hesitated a moment, then nodded. I sucked an ounce of hope out of that. A nod was good. I could build on that.

Of course, it also meant I was back at ground zero, having to start over, building something I had thought was already standing.

⌖

THERE'S NO TORTURE quite so fine as having to make people think you still belong to someone when you're not sure yourself.

I told Gillian what a wonderful time we'd had at the beach, hoping she wouldn't ask why I'd come back to school without having dinner with Callum first. And when she popped a DVD into her Mac with its seventeen-inch screen, I didn't complain when it was Jackie Chan and Owen Wilson. I was just thankful that for two hours I didn't have to talk about Callum.

Monday morning I went to the dining room at the last possible minute and snagged a yogurt, then timed it so I got to math class after I saw Callum and Brett go in.

And I got my reward. He smiled at me.

I smiled back as though we'd spent the last twelve hours in romantic bliss and slid into my seat feeling as though the sun had come out and a gospel choir had just swung into the "Hallelujah Chorus" in the back of the room.

I'd never say another word about our relationship to anyone again. From now on, we'd have a total cone of silence over us, and what happened inside would stay inside. Wild horses wouldn't drag our secrets out of me, so that—

"Lissa!" Vanessa grabbed my arm and hustled me into the nearest empty room. "We have to talk."

I looked around at the maps and the diagrams of the earth's crust. The Earth Sciences classroom.

"What's up?"

She threw her arms around me in a victory hug. "You are so amazing for getting Angelina for us!"

Grinning, I hugged her back. "No problem. She'll fly in, do our gig, and fly out again. My mom's taking care of it. We can send the donation later."

"Utterly cool. I love it when people take things off my plate and just deal with them. Not that I wouldn't delegate getting her a limo and stuff. But now I don't have to."

I glanced around. "So is that why you dragged me in here?"

"No, silly. That was just props in person for a job well done. I dragged you in here to tell you something massive."

"You and Brett."

She blinked at me. "You just found out about that?"

"Callum told me yesterday."

She waved it off. "Oh, yeah. We've been together for a while now. Totally meant to be. Which is kind of a nice segue to what I want to tell you."

I couldn't imagine what she and Brett had to do with me, unless she was going to propose a double date or something corny like that. "What?"

"Well, you know his family has this sublime winery up in Napa."

A number of restaurants, some prime chunks of San Francisco real estate. A trust fund. A winery did not surprise me a bit. "Okay."

"We've been dying to get some time alone, away from this dive, so we decided to go up for a getaway. We're leaving after class on Friday."

Wait a second. "But what about the ball?"

"What about it? We'll only be gone Friday night. We're totally skipping the guest tours and parental stuff, but I'll be back by three or so on Saturday to start getting ready. You should see my dress. No one will have anything like it."

No one would have anything like my silver-and-white waterfall dress, either.

"I can't wait to see it," I said. "Well, I need to go. Have a great time at the vineyard."

"No, wait." She put a hand on my wrist. "I haven't told you yet. I was thinking about what you said the other night in my room."

"Vanessa, I'd rather we didn't—"

"And here's the plan. I know how hard it is to get time alone with your man. Callum's living at home. You have a roommate. You never get any privacy, because wherever you go, people are always watching."

"Well—"

"Believe me, I know. I can never wear the same thing twice when I go out. The paparazzi are a total pain."

"But—"

"So here's the thing. It's perfect. I don't have a roommate this term, and I'll be gone Friday night. I'll leave my spare key with you, and you and Callum can use my room!"

Her eyes sparkled as if she'd just given me the best present ever.

I didn't know what to say. "Wow, um, that's very generous of you—but I don't think—"

With a wave of her hand, she shut me up. No loss. My brain and my mouth refused to connect, mostly because this was so out there on so many levels I didn't know where to start.

"Don't worry about Callum. He'll totally go for it. Even if a girl gets that far with him, it's hard for him to take her home. Nine times out of ten, if he thinks the coast is clear, somebody shows up and totally spoils the moment. But this way, you're guaranteed no interruptions." She grinned. "Even if I forget my hair dryer, I promise I won't come back."

Now was not the time to break the news that Callum was mad at me and my whole Benefactors' Day weekend was in jeopardy.

"But guys aren't allowed in the girls' dorm," I said, sounding lame even to myself. Girls like Vanessa paid no attention to rules. She'd just think I was a little teacher's pet for caring. But after the concealed alcohol episode, I did care. I didn't want to get expelled and sent somewhere that meant I'd never see Callum again.

Again the airy wave of the hand Vanessa used to dispense with objections. Like a magic wand. She ignored them, thus they had no reality. "Pfft. I'm on the ground floor. Callum can come in the window. Easy. No one needs to know he was there."

Except me. And Vanessa. And, undoubtedly, Brett Loyola. And how would Callum handle that? How would he feel about being set up for a romantic rendezvous? Would he see it as his lifelong friend trying to help, or as totally aggro interference that would break us up for good?

As I followed Vanessa out the door, I came to the only conclusion I could.

I had to ask him. I had to risk it. I had to do something to mend this chasm between us, and if that meant making him an offer he couldn't refuse, then I'd do it.

Spending the rest of the school year as another one of Callum's exes would be infinitely worse.

LMansfield	Can we talk?
CMcCloud	OK.
LMansfield	Grab a sandwich and meet me on side lawn?
CMcCloud	What's up?
LMansfield	A surprise.
CMcCloud	Good or bad?
LMansfield	It's good to be bad.

chapter 22

THE CHICKEN SALAD and avocado sandwich felt like paste in my mouth as I watched Callum cross the lawn. I took a quick swallow of Odwalla pomegranate juice and hoped I didn't have tarragon in my teeth as I smiled up at him from my seat on the grass.

"Hey." He sprawled next to me and investigated the contents of his own sandwich.

No smile, no kiss. I may as well have been one of the guys.

I visualized the two of us whirling onto the dance floor and took courage.

"I'm sorry I made you mad yesterday," I said. "It won't happen again."

"What won't?"

"Me talking to people about us."

He looked a little lost, as if this hadn't been what he was expecting. "Oh. Okay. That's good."

"What did you think I was going to say?"

He shrugged and took an enormous bite of his sandwich. He'd

picked the roast beef. Typical. "Nothing. Stuff at home stinks. I'm kinda stressed about it."

I went straight into Concerned Girlfriend mode. "Want to talk about it? Can I help?"

He shook his head and frowned, as though that was the last solution he'd pick. "Talking about it wrecks my mood. So." He brightened a little. "What's all this about being good to be bad?"

"Promise you won't be mad."

"Okay."

"Vanessa came to me with this totally illegal plan. You'll laugh."

"Probably. She comes up with some whacked ideas. And they usually are illegal."

"She and Brett are going to Napa Friday night. And she's leaving her room key with me in case I want to use it."

He finished his sandwich and glanced at me. "What for? You need a quiet place to study?"

Yes, that was so my image. Me, giving up a Friday night to hit the books.

"No." With one finger, I smoothed a stray lock of hair away from his chin. "I was thinking more of having some privacy with you."

Now his gaze locked on me for real. "Privacy. Because Vanessa doesn't have a roommate."

"And I do. And because she doesn't have a family."

"And I do." He was silent for a moment. "That's some plan."

"Illegal, but effective."

"What do you want to do?"

Dance with you at the Benefactors' Day ball. Meet your family as your girlfriend. Spend the term with you. Spend the holidays with you.

Build a relationship, one thing at a time. And first things first.

"What do *you* want to do?" I said carefully.

"What do you think?" There was that sexy grin again, after a long absence.

I was back in the game.

⟡

"YOU ARE SO not going to do that." Gillian's hands dropped from the harp's strings and an unfinished chord hung in the air, waiting for resolution. "Are you?"

I couldn't very well disappear on Friday night and have her call out Security, thinking I'd been abducted. And I didn't want to lie about what I was doing, either. I'm a terrible liar—the thin-skinned, blushing, hopeless kind who always gets found out.

"I have to." How could I explain this so that look would leave Gillian's face, and yet not break my promise to Callum that I wouldn't talk about him behind his back? "Today at lunch was the first time he spoke to me since we had a little fight yesterday. We need some time together. And that's impossible to get around here without some kind of miracle."

"You could always go out," she observed.

"And do what? Sit in his car? There are always people around in restaurants and theaters."

"If you're just talking, what's the big deal? That's what people do in restaurants and theaters."

"Maybe we don't want to just talk."

"Uh-huh. At least you wouldn't get arrested."

"I know—" I stopped, a second after I realized she was being sarcastic. "Don't be a *mo guai nuer.*"

She snorted. "There's being an MGN and being honest. I just think you're going at this the wrong way."

"Oh, like you know so much about it. I don't see the guys breaking our door down to get to you." Although I had seen her in the Physics lab a couple more times, talking with Lucas Hayes. Maybe something had gotten going at the prayer circle after I'd left.

Gillian looked down at the strings and plucked a red one. Middle C hung in the air. "Maybe the guys interested in me have more finesse. Maybe some of us use brains and conversation, not our bodies, to keep a guy that way."

"What are you insinuating?"

"Nothing. I'm just saying, I'm hearing too much about sex and not very much about who Callum is and stuff you do together, that's all."

"Maybe I don't want to talk about it. He hates when people talk behind his back."

She pulled a blue string, and a fourth interval vibrated quietly before she put her hand on the strings to still them. "Telling your roomie what you did on a date isn't talking behind his back. Is he paranoid, or what?"

"No!" My voice reverberated like the string, and I took a breath to calm down. "People at our level are visible, that's all. Other people like to talk about us because they don't have anything else to talk about. Students, reporters—it's all the same."

"'Our level'?"

I nodded. "Callum is oil money. You told me that yourself. Brett Loyola is from this old San Francisco family that owns tons of real estate. Vanessa's family is in politics, not to mention her semi-royal mom. My family's in the movie business, and my mom's family is in banking and retail. The point is, they have enough trouble with the paparazzi reporting on their every move in public without their friends yakking it up about their private ones."

"Gosh. Banking. I guess I wouldn't know anything about that, being from Chinatown and all."

I stared at her. Was she being straight or sarcastic? Never mind.

"The point is, I promised him I wouldn't talk about us. I only told you about Friday so you wouldn't freak and report me as a missing person."

"Gee, thanks. I *so* would have done that."

"Gillian, knock off the sarcasm, would you?"

She pushed the harp to the side and got up. "I don't get how a person so nice can be so self-destructive."

I stared at her. "What?"

"Look at you. You come in here and tell me point-blank you're planning to (a) break school rules by letting a guy into the girls' dorm, and (b) break a promise to God by spending the night with him. Don't you hear what you're saying?"

"I'm not breaking my promise *or* spending the night," I said as patiently as I could. "We're spending the evening together. And if he never leaves Vanessa's room, what difference does it make to the rest of the dorm?"

"Listen to yourself! What difference does it make to me, knowing what you're doing and wondering if I should tell Tobin? Huh? Did you think about the position you're putting me in?"

"I hope it isn't the one called 'rat.' "

She rolled her eyes. "Great. First I'm an MGN, now I'm a rat."

"I said I *hope* it isn't. But if you think you should tell Ms. Tobin, then that's what you have to do."

"Don't be a martyr."

I'm not an angry person. My temper has a long leash, and I only lose it a couple of times a year. Despite my best efforts, this was working up to being one of those times. "I'm not. I'm just saying, you have to do what you think is right."

"Like you're doing? Lissa, did it ever occur to you to pray about this?"

"I have been praying."

"Then you must not be listening to the answer. Because if you were, you couldn't do it. God won't tempt us more than we can bear, but all bets are off when we deliberately book a room and walk into it."

"You're insinuating again. Come on. Spit out what you really mean."

"I mean, are you going to give up your virginity on Friday night?"

"No, of course not. I told you. I keep my promises."

"So you're just going to be the world's biggest tease? What is that going to say to Callum about Christian girls?"

Something in the region of my heart stretched past the breaking point, snapping like a rubber band.

"That's enough. I've listened to you, and you've done nothing but insult me. I'm out of here."

I grabbed my wallet out of my tote and hit the door practically at a run. As it swung shut behind me, I heard a discordant sound shiver through the air, as if Gillian had whacked the strings of her harp with the flat of her hand.

Ha. Good thing she wasn't anywhere near *my* hand. I'd show her a thing or two about discord.

I didn't really care where I went. Walking at workout speed, I crossed the lawn and headed downhill. I could have gone to Callum's house, but then I'd have to tell him why I was upset, which would mean confessing that I'd talked about him with Gillian in spite of my promise.

He was right. I should have kept my mouth shut and let her call Security. They'd never have thought to look in Vanessa's room, would they? I'd have been safe. And now it was too late for that plan.

Somehow my subconscious directed me down Fillmore Street to the Starbucks, where I ordered a nice, soothing caramel macchiato. And since I needed major soothing, I made it a venti.

As I walked back up the street, looking in the shop windows, most of which had closed earlier in the evening, my phone rang, deep in the pocket of my blue school blazer.

"Hey, Gremmie Girl," Kaz said.

"Not." I grinned at the name he'd called me when I first started surfing. "I'll beat you to the waves any day."

"Ha. Not in Fog City, you won't."

"I'll have you know I was at the beach yesterday."

"Yeah? How's it lookin'?"

"Beautiful. Not too crowded, either. I have to get my stuff from Dad's." Callum didn't have surf racks, but the board might fit inside if we wedged it between the seats of his Prius.

"Did you go with the boyfriend?"

"Yes. We had a great time."

"Are you with him now? Did I interrupt something?"

"No. Relax." I sighed. "I had a fight with my roommate and I'm walking it off with a caramel macchiato."

"A fight? With the pretty Asian chick?"

What, like somehow the two didn't go together? "The sarcastic, name-calling Asian chick, you mean?"

"Yow. Catfight!"

"Shut up. You're supposed to be on my side."

"I am. Totally." His voice lost the laughter and became gentle. Which was good, because I could really, really use gentle right about then. "What'd you fight about?"

I was not going to compound my broken promises by telling him. "Nothing. It was stupid."

"Didn't sound stupid to me."

"It—" I stopped. "What?"

"Confession time. I just got off the phone with her."

I stopped walking and checked to make sure I was still holding my coffee and not dropping it on the sidewalk in shock. "With Gillian?"

"She's worried sick about you."

"She is not. She's a flippin' backstabber, is what she is. She had no business blabbing about my personal stuff to you."

"Because I'm only your oldest friend."

"Right!"

Silence.

"Awkward," he said at last. "If you really want me to butt out, I guess I'll just shut up and go away."

"No, don't do that," I said on a long sigh. "I'm sorry. It's just that I promised Callum I wouldn't talk about him with my friends, and now I'm breaking my promise right and left."

"Why'd he make you promise that?"

I gave him the same explanation I'd given Gillian.

He snorted in derision. "Lame, man. Lame. He just doesn't want the witnesses blabbing about his bad behavior, that's all."

"Look, I know you don't like him on principle, but that's just not true."

"Wanna bet? He's all over this plan to take over this girl's room, making you an accessory to broken rules littering the place. And then what does he plan to do with you? Go for the big one—the broken promise to God."

Ow, straight to the solar plexus. "No! You've got it totally wrong!"

"Liss, look at this straight, okay? If this were right, would we even be talking about broken rules and broken promises? How can God be anywhere near this situation, if all we can see is bad stuff trailing it like afterburn from *Serenity*'s engines?"

I was not in the mood to trade movie metaphors, no matter how old and well-loved. "You're overreacting. You just can't be happy for me because I'm in love with somebody else."

"You're not in love, Liss. Love makes you do good things." He paused. "This is lust, baby."

I was just about to use up my year's quota of temper. "Don't tell me how I feel."

"Someone has to. Since when did you get so desperate, Liss? You never used to be like this. Even with that idiot Aidan, you were still running the show."

"Maybe that's why he dumped me."

"And maybe that's why a dozen guys stood in line when they heard he did. If you were here right now, you could pick and choose. The point is, you don't have to go begging to anyone, girl."

A pang hit me. "Don't call me that."

"Uh, memory check—I've been calling you that since junior high."

"It's what Callum calls me."

"Oh. Well. Wouldn't want to trespass on his noun."

For some reason, I felt tears prickle in my throat. "Don't be mean, Kaz. I need you to support me."

"I'm sorry." His voice filled with gentleness again, instead of that aggressive humor he could use like a weapon. "I do support you. One hundred percent. I just don't support what you're doing. I think it's a mistake."

"Showing love to someone is a mistake?"

"No, if you keep it right. But, like I said, there's a lot of wrong following this around. Can't you do something different?"

"Like what?"

"Bake him cookies?"

"Kaz . . ."

"I dunno. You make the best chocolate-chip oatmeal cookies in the 'verse."

"Not helping."

"You gotta pray, Liss," he said, turning serious.

"This isn't exactly something the Creator of the 'verse—and I don't mean Joss Whedon—needs to get involved in."

"Maybe it'll help you see a different trajectory."

Again, the vision of Callum and me whirling in the spotlight flashed onto the screen in my mind, the only couple in the darkened ballroom.

"Maybe." I took a sip of cooling coffee and began to trudge up the hill. "I gotta go, Kaz. This is, like, a thirty-degree slope and I can't talk and climb at the same time."

"Okay. Take care of yourself, girl."

"I will."

"I'll be praying for ya. For vision. For resolution."

I said good-bye and pocketed the phone. Resolution? Who needed that?

I'd already resolved what I was going to do. Nothing Kaz said—to the Lord or anybody else—was going to change that.

chapter 23

ONCE THE FLOOR monitor gave the all-clear, Ms. Tobin chased the last student out of the common room and shut off the lights downstairs. Lying on Vanessa's bed, I watched the strip of light under the door wink out, leaving me with only the glow of the candles I'd lit on the dresser, the computer table, and the second windowsill. The first window was clear and standing open a few inches. Vanessa's computer sat open on the desk, but I didn't mess with it. And no matter how big the temptation, I didn't look in her closet, either.

My territory was right here, on the bed.

I had sodas chilling in her little fridge and a bag of chips, a box of Oreos, and some sliced fruit laid out on a tray on the second bed. I didn't know what kind of movie Callum would be in the mood for, so I'd brought my beloved *Firefly* DVDs, *Pirates of the Caribbean 3*, and the newest *X-Men* to cover all the bases.

Four days after our last conversation, Gillian still wasn't talking to me. I'd expected an apology and gotten nothing, and until she was ready to say she was sorry for the things she'd said, I was just as happy not to hear from her. I needed support, not preaching.

And as for Kaz, it had been nice to hear he supported me, but the rest I could do without.

It wasn't like I was falling into bed with Callum. Okay, strictly speaking, the bed was the only place where we could sit together, oversized pillows being what they were, but we weren't going to sleep there or anything. All we wanted to do was grab a little privacy. Where, I ask you, was the big sin in that?

All the same, every nerve in my body felt energized, as though a high-voltage current were running through all of them. It wasn't fear, exactly. It was more like major anticipation edged with a little bit of danger.

When the hedge outside the window rustled and I heard tap-tap-tap on the glass, my heart jumped against my ribs. I rolled off the bed and held the curtain aside as Callum pushed open the window. He sat on the sill, swung his legs over, and dropped to the floor.

When I turned from locking it again and making sure the curtains had no cracks, the sight of him made that melting sensation happen inside me, the way it always did.

"Hey, girl." He held out his arms and I went into them without a word. This was where I belonged.

"You smell good," I said against his shirt front.

"You look good. New dress?"

I shook my head. "An old favorite."

"It's going to be hard to get you out of."

"Ahem." Maybe I should clarify exactly what *having some privacy* meant. "You're getting ahead of yourself. Want a soda?"

"Sure."

I pulled one out of the fridge and handed it to him. "I have munchies and a bunch of movies, too."

"All set for a pajama party."

He made it sound like I was twelve, and that was the last impression I wanted. I didn't want him to see me as a kid, but at the same time, losing the clothes wasn't exactly on the agenda. At least, I didn't think it was.

"Cookies?"

He put his hands loosely on my waist. "Why would I want to waste time eating?"

There just wasn't a good answer to that except the one I gave— a kiss. A geological epoch could have passed while I stood there kissing Callum and I wouldn't have noticed. When he finally let me go, he leaned over and blew out the candles, leaving only the ones on the dresser burning. The room fell into a romantic, sepia darkness that erased all traces of Vanessa and just left us at the edges of the flickering light.

He led me to the bed, but in the dimness I ran my foot into the stack of movies on the floor.

"Ooh!" I said in surprise, and he waited as I kicked them out of our path. Then we sat together on the bed and he kissed me again.

In his eyes I saw my dreams coming true. His focus on me was absolute. After this, we'd be a couple for sure. You couldn't share moments like this without it changing you forever.

I leaned back on the pillow and he followed me. And then I was lost in him, in the things he whispered to me, the things I murmured back, until all that existed was Callum and the dark.

chapter 24

WHEN I WOKE in my own room Saturday morning, I felt drugged.

I'd tiptoed in sometime after two, and a bleary glance at the clock told me I'd awakened a good four hours too soon. I rolled over and snuggled under the comforter, touching my lips with a finger. They'd had more of a workout last night than they'd had in six months. Aidan had been really hot, but he wasn't much of a kisser. And I wasn't, of course, in the habit of kissing Kaz, the only other guy I spent time with.

Guh. Why was I thinking of Aidan and Kaz right now? I should be sinking back into dreamland and reprising last night.

Sometime later, right when I was getting to the good part, someone grabbed me by the shoulder. "Lissa!"

I shrugged it off and mumbled, pulling the duvet over my head. It got ripped off me. "Lissa, wake up!"

Irritation flooded me and I finally cracked my eyes open. Gillian stood next to my bed. When I got my glasses on, I could see she was fully dressed in jeans and a bright red T-shirt advertising some choir called the Gospel Grrls. Didn't she know that was against the rules?

"What?" I said, halfway between a snap and a whine, as I sat up.

"You gotta see this. Look." She took my face between her hands and turned it to her notebook, which was sitting on my desk next to the bed.

The screen was dark. "What? Gillian, I need to sleep. Go away."

"Watch it."

The tension in her tone finally got through to me. With a sigh, I turned so I could see better.

"There's nothing there."

"Yes, there is. Wait."

Music began, some kind of slow hip-hop beat. And then a tall blond girl with hair as long as mine walked into the frame. Scene change. Callum walked in. *Whoa.*

What? Wait a second.

They turned and kissed, and suddenly some layer of disbelief peeled off my brain and I realized what I was looking at.

Myself.

"Wh—wh—"

"It gets worse," Gillian said grimly.

Someone had cut the scenes so they were timed perfectly with the hookup going on in the song. I saw Callum blow out the candles. Saw myself fall back on the bed. And then the music came up and supplied all the missing information.

Clip. Edit. Clip. The song ended, and then in the silence I heard my own voice go "Ooh!" as if . . . as if I'd . . .

Oh, no. No, that hadn't happened. We hadn't—I hadn't—

Cold horror cascaded over me like a bucket of ice water down my back. My hands began to shake. My cheeks felt cold as the color drained away. "This isn't happening," I said. "It's not real."

"It is. It's on the school server, which has been feeding it to all the PA screens in the classrooms and common rooms." Gillian bit off her syllables as though they were crackers. "Everyone at breakfast knew about it because it started playing when the dining room opened at nine."

"No." Denial.

"Curzon had it stopped, but it was too late. Half the kids in school have it downloaded already, and the other half are watching."

"No." Bargaining.

"Lissa, saying that isn't going to help."

"But how? How did—"

I swung my feet out of bed, pulled the notebook onto my lap, and played the movie again. It hadn't changed. If anything, it looked worse now that horror had swept my brain crystal clear. Candlelight illuminated an arm, a leg, a swath of my hair. You couldn't see what was going on very clearly (oh, thank you, Callum, for blowing out most of the candles), but over the music you could hear—and that was just as bad. And worst of all was that "Ooh!" dubbed in at the end.

I looked up at Gillian. "I swear to you, that isn't what you think. I knocked over a bunch of DVDs. The whole thing is a manip. It didn't happen."

With a sigh, Gillian sat next to me and took the instrument of torture away. "Something must have happened to give them footage to work with."

Those beautiful moments with Callum seemed to burn away at the edges, leaving me with nothing but the way other people would see them. How could I have been so stupid? How could I have walked into this with my eyes wide open and yet been so completely blind?

My stomach rolled, and I wondered if a person could actually be sick from shame.

"You don't believe me." Somehow, that made me feel even worse.

"More like, I don't get you." She closed the notebook, then

glanced at me. "I don't get why you deliberately went against your beliefs and what you knew was right. Maybe you didn't break your promise to keep your purity—I don't know and you don't have to tell me. But you sure put it in jeopardy."

I'd expected judgment in that gaze, and maybe there was, a little. But mostly I saw the tears that she blinked back. For me.

"I didn't expect *this*." I put my head in my hands, close to tears myself. "If you say I brought it on myself, so help me . . ."

Silence. And it spoke volumes.

Maybe we were both trying not to choke up. Or maybe she was giving me a chance to tell myself the truth.

I *had* brought it on myself. I'd made stupid choices. I'd gone ahead and done what I wanted instead of going to God and asking Him what He wanted. And now look.

"Nobody deserves to be broadcast on the school system," Gillian said at last. "I guess the only thing we can do is try to find out how she did it."

"Who?"

"Vanessa, of course."

"No, no. She would never—we're friends."

"Is that what you call it? Then how did this get recorded? By astral projection?"

"I don't know." I tipped over and buried my face in the pillow. "I want to crawl away and never come back."

"No, you don't. You want to find out who did this."

"What difference does it make?"

"Lissa, think. The picture is shot from the end of the bed. All these rooms are laid out the same way. The v-cam had to be somewhere between the desk and the wardrobe."

A suffocating cloud of humiliation and hurt lay on me as heavily as a down duvet on an August afternoon. What point was there in all this? It was a little late for the private-eye act.

"Lissa?"

"Go away." I pulled the pillow over my head.

She yanked it off. "You have to think. You have to get through this. You might be able to hide in here today, but you'll have to come out Monday morning and face everyone. Not to mention—"

A knock sounded at the door and Gillian froze.

"Miss Mansfield? Miss Chang? Open the door, please."

"It's Curzon!" Gillian hissed, like I hadn't figured that out already. "Here." She threw the hoodie that had been hanging over my desk chair at me, and I leaped to the dresser and yanked on a pair of pajama bottoms. Once I was dressed in more than a T-shirt, she opened the door.

The headmistress stepped in, dressed in her blue blazer with its gold badge on the breast, and a long skirt made of the school plaid instead of the habitual short blue one.

I stared at her, trying to figure out why she'd be all dressed up at ten o'clock on a Saturday morning. And then I remembered.

Benefactors' Day. She was ready to receive all the dignitaries as they arrived. To show the parents around and make them proud of what their tuition was paying for.

Parents.

Oh, Lord, help me. What were Mom and Dad going to say?

My insides felt like they were about to cave in, and before I could stop them, tears spilled down my cheeks.

"Miss Mansfield," she said. "Lissa."

Her voice held such kindness that I gasped—a single sob that I couldn't control.

"I see that you've seen the video," she said. I hung my head, unable to look at her. *Dui bu chi.* "I've had it pulled from the server, and we're investigating how such a thing could have been uploaded, given the password structure."

"The incoming computer science class hacks into the server every fall," Gillian said. "It's like a rite of passage. Anybody could have had the password."

"Is that so?" Ms. Curzon looked over her glasses at Gillian. "Interesting. In any case, I'm most concerned now about how the video was created in the first place. Lissa, leaving all other details aside for the moment, I'm assuming you had no knowledge that you were being filmed."

I still couldn't speak. Fear and grief were lodged in my throat like a big lump of peanut butter. So I shook my head no.

"We were just trying to figure out how they did it," Gillian put in. "Given the continuous angle of the shot, it was a stationary camera somewhere here." She waved a hand toward the desk, where the sleeping notebook sat, and the wardrobe behind it.

My throat cleared abruptly. "We were in Vanessa's room. She had a notebook, too. Sitting right there."

"Webcam," Gillian said immediately. "You couldn't tell it was on?"

I shook my head. "I didn't want to mess with her stuff. The screen was dark. It never occurred to me that it was on—or that she would—"

"We don't yet know for sure it was Miss Talbot, given that she was and is off campus," the headmistress said, "but we'll certainly investigate."

"They've probably already wiped the file," Gillian offered. "The IT guy could probably find its footprint, though. And maybe the port it was uploaded through, if you get the notebook's IP addy. The server will have a record."

"All excellent suggestions," Ms. Curzon said. "In the meantime, Lissa, I know this is painful, but do you have an explanation for the origin of the movie?"

"She was set up," Gillian said at once.

Curzon looked at her. "I asked Lissa, Miss Chang."

"Sorry, ma'am." Gillian subsided, but stayed on high alert. If I hadn't been so miserable, I might have appreciated her willingness to help me. Especially after the lousy way I'd been treating her all week.

The fact that she'd been right about my bad choices—and that Kaz had been right about Callum, and that even my sister had been right about dating someone who didn't believe—did not help.

Compounding my mistakes by lying about them just seemed stupid. I was already finished at Spencer Academy. Being expelled for breaking the rules would be a mercy. If I was, I could be out of here by tomorrow and wouldn't have to face the laughter and jeers on Monday.

Happy, happy thought.

I lifted my head. "Vanessa loaned me her room so that I could have some privacy with Callum," I said. "I know it's against the rules to bring a boy into the dorm, ma'am. I'm fine with being expelled."

"You are, are you?" She lifted a brow. "And who is going to escort our celebrity guest this evening?"

"Vanessa can do it." She'd totally be in her element. Me, crushed forever in ignominy, kicked out of school, and Angelina at her side. It would be the apex of her junior year—and we were only in the first term. "I can pack my stuff and be out of here by noon."

"You worry me," she said. "Once again I find you alarmingly anxious to be punished."

"This time I really deserve it." *Get on with it so I can get out of here, would you?*

I could take a cab to Dad's and then revisit the boarding-school versus live-in discussion. Being by myself with only one other person sounded like heaven. I could go back to our house on the hillside in Santa Barbara with its cool sandstone and quiet, sleepy gardens and pick up where I'd left off. It was still only first term. People would hardly have had time to notice I'd been gone.

"Unless it involves blood, fire, or illegal substances, we don't expel on the first infraction," Curzon said slowly. "I'm afraid we're going to have to come up with an alternative. A month's detention under the supervision of the cleaning staff should be sufficient."

I gaped at her. Not be expelled?

Oh, no. No, no. I had to be expelled. Immediately. Today.

"But this is my second infraction."

"You were not actually proven to be guilty of the first. I'm afraid that Newton's Law applies in real life. In this case, the reaction to your actions is very unfortunate, and I'll do my best to find out who posted that video. You are simply going to have to live through the consequences. It seems to me that punishment is quite severe enough." She crossed to the door. "But for the record, as I said, a month's detention, assisting the cleaning staff. You'll report to Mrs. Dumfries, whose office you can find on the ground floor behind Admissions, after classes on Monday. In the meantime, ladies, I very much look forward to seeing you both at the festivities today, and at the ball this evening."

With a smile, the headmistress turned on the heel of her—I blinked—Doc Marten Mary Janes??—and left.

I looked at Gillian in appeal. "They have to expel me. Think of something involving blood."

"They'd just have you committed, not expelled."

I jumped up and gripped the windowsill as I peered out, searching the view. "What can I burn? A tree? A building? How come everything out there is made of stone?"

"Lissa. Calm down."

I whirled. "You don't get it! I have to get out of here."

"Run away? And let them win?"

"They already have."

Gillian guided me back to the bed and tried to get me to sit, but I couldn't. I bounced up and began to pace.

"For once in my life I wish I knew someone who dealt drugs."

"Like that would improve the situation."

"It would get me out!" Six steps up. Six back. I wrapped the hoodie around myself, protecting myself, warding off the future.

"And tossed in jail. Here." She stopped me by wrapping both arms around me from behind, and steered me back to the bed. "This is what we should do."

Oh, thank you. A plan. Gillian would come up with something. It might not involve blood, drugs, or fire, but she would help me.

"Father God," she said firmly, sitting beside me, "we really need You right now."

That much was true. I didn't so much bow my head as hang it. My shoulders drooped, and I gave myself up to what I should have done ages ago: prayer. Real prayer. Not visualizing a fantasy and calling it prayer.

Guh. How bullheaded, blind, and downright stupid could I be?

The problem was, how could I come to God when I'd deliberately turned my back on Him and done what I wanted? How could I ask for help and forgiveness now, when I didn't deserve it?

I couldn't see my way to a place where I could do that. So I sat there and let Gillian say it for me.

"Father, whatever Lissa did is between You and her," Gillian went on. "We come to You now asking for strength to get through what's coming. No matter what, we belong to You, and we know that You're sufficient for us. No matter how dumb we act, You still love us. Please forgive Lissa for disappointing You, and forgive me for not showing love to her when I should have. Help us, Lord. We sincerely need it."

"Amen," I said. Then I turned to her. "I'm sorry I was such an MGN."

"I wasn't there for you when you needed me. I got my pride hurt. I'm sorry, too. What are you going to do now?"

I glanced at the floor next to the bed. "Pray some more. And take a shower. And call my parents and tell them before they get here at noon and Curzon does it for me."

"That sounds like fun."

"What's the worst that could happen?"

The words were no sooner out of my mouth than my iPhone chimed.

"If that's Callum, I hope you tell him to kiss off and bark at the moon," Gillian said. My friend. Always the perfect lady.

"It's probably Kaz." Though why he'd call to get an update on an event he'd hated even thinking about, I had no idea.

A glance at the display told the truth. "Hey, Mom."

"Lissa, this is a disaster."

I shot an agonized glance at Gillian. Great. Curzon had already broken the news. "Mom, I'm sorry. I'm so sorry. I let you down and I'm just going to have to get through it. Try to survive, you know?"

"No, no, darling, it's me who's let you down."

"What?"

"Obviously someone has already called and told you. Oh, sweetie, if I could have done something, I would have, but you know how she is."

"I sure do now."

"Or maybe you don't," my mother rushed on. "The kids come first, which I can hardly blame her for, but after giving me a commitment . . . I knew how disappointed you were going to be."

I frowned. "Wait. Mom. Whoa. What are you talking about? Did Ms. Curzon call you?"

"No, darling. What does she have to do with Angelina bailing on us?"

I sat down suddenly and hard. Good thing the bed was there. "Angelina bailed?" My voice went up the scale and off the chart.

"That's what I've been saying. One of the children was admitted to the hospital with a virus of some kind, and you know her. She'd no more go to a benefit with a child in the hospital than jump off a building."

"She's not coming," I repeated, as though I might have gotten it wrong. "We have no celebrity guest."

"That's right." Mom said something else, but that stifling quilt of fear and humiliation had me in its grip again.

First the video.

Now no celebrity.

Suddenly drugs, blood, and fire were looking really good. Preferably all at once.

chapter 25

I HAD NO CHOICE. Whether she'd set me up or not, Vanessa had to know about Angelina ASAP.

So instead of hiding in the shower until I was wrinkled and pink, I got on with it. As I dried my hair, I thought about French braiding it, then decided not to. It would come in handy as a personal curtain if the laughter got too loud. I got dressed in my uniform and found Vanessa's cell number.

She didn't answer until the fourth ring, and I refused to let my imagination dwell on what she and Brett might be doing on a Saturday morning in the wine country.

Probably not having a *Sound of Music* moment in the hills.

"Why are you calling me here?" she asked when she found out it was me.

"We have a problem."

"Honestly, Lissa. Deal with it. I'm kind of unavailable here."

"It's a serious problem," I said doggedly. "Angelina bailed."

"What?" Like mine, her voice spiked into a squeak. "Why?"

"One of her kids is in the hospital. My mom just called me to say it's not going to happen."

"Okay. Okay. Regroup." I pictured her with a palm pressed to her forehead. "What's your Plan B?"

"I don't have a Plan B."

"What do you mean? Every benefit has a Plan B. That's, like, Event Planning 101."

I guess. If you've been doing this since junior high, like some people. "I don't have one. Once we got Angelina, I thought I was done." I was really done now. "What about DeLayne? She's heading up PR, right? Maybe she's got one." It wasn't like she'd given me any help with the guest, anyway.

Vanessa went off on me like an atomic bomb, screaming and calling me names, most of which weren't anatomically possible. But how was this my fault, I ask you? I didn't know I was supposed to have an understudy in reserve, hanging around waiting to be called on set when the A-list talent didn't show. Maybe that was standard procedure in Vanessa's world, but it sure wasn't in mine.

She finished with a threat, shrieked at the top of the phone's upper register. "You'd better find someone before I get back, or so help me—" She stopped to take a breath and I grabbed the opportunity.

"Or what? You can't possibly do anything worse than you've already done."

"What. Are. You. Talking. About?"

"Oh, I think you know, Vanessa."

"Enlighten me, O brainless one."

"The webcam? The video? I know it was you. I just want you to know there will be consequences."

Not that I had a clue what they'd be, but no one could be that cruel and not have it come back to bite them. Someday, somewhere, Vanessa would have to pay up.

"I have no idea what you're talking about, you incompetent loon. And if you're threatening me, I'd use your other brain cell and think twice before you get a visit from my father's legal team."

I opened my mouth to call her something choice, and then caught myself. Praying one second and screaming swear words the next? Did I want to be a hypocrite like Vanessa, acting like a friend and then smiling as I deliberately hurt someone? Or did I want to be the person God had called me to be three years ago?

"It's not a threat," I said quietly. "Just a reality."

I disconnected, having gotten nothing out of that conversation but a tiny victory . . . and the last word.

For the first time I realized I was alone in the room. Gillian must have left while I was in the shower, which meant I had no one to fume to about how horrible Vanessa was.

Like Gillian didn't know.

I slipped the phone into my pocket and got out a piece of paper. Okay, so who did I know who'd be willing to come and guest at a benefit in—I glanced at my watch—nine hours? Particularly when Angelina's name and not theirs had been printed over the title in the program?

When the door opened fifteen minutes later, my sheet of paper was still empty. But I saw, as my spirits tried to get up off the metaphorical floor, that Gillian's and Carly's hands were not.

"We raided the dining room before it closed," Carly said. "We thought you'd like oatmeal best, but it was all gone."

"Ha ha," I said as she and Gillian laid out fruit, bagels, strawberry cream cheese, and paper cups of coffee on Gillian's desk. "You guys deserve a medal."

"We were hungry." Gillian knocked back a gulp of coffee. "And hanging around the caf listening to all the static about the video just made me barf."

"There weren't that many people." Carly was so nice, trying to be encouraging. "The room was maybe half full."

"The other half are probably at their computers, sending it to all their day-student friends." With a sense of doom, I bit into a thickly spread bagel. My stomach still felt unsteady, as if I were on a boat in a heavy chop, but that could be because I hadn't eaten yet. Well, the food would stay down or it wouldn't. If these guys were kind enough to bring it here so I wouldn't have to face the dining room, then I'd eat it in gratitude, even if I lost it later.

"Do you think Callum has heard?" Carly asked a little hesitantly. Maybe she thought I'd be mad if she butted in with a personal question. The girl had brought me food. Done what little she could to make a ghastly situation better. She could ask anything she wanted.

I lifted a shoulder. "I don't know. He's a day student, so he's at home."

The two of them glanced at each other. I caught it. "What? What's that look?"

"He's downstairs in the common room," Gillian said at last.

I caught my breath. "And? What's he doing? Who's he with?"

"Those guys," Carly said. "Rory Stapleton and Todd, and DeLayne Geary's brother."

But not Brett hung at the end of her sentence, but I had other things to think about.

"Did he look upset? Is he going totally darkside on them?"

Callum would come to my defense. I didn't have any kind of clout at Spencer, but he was *numero uno*. If he said, "Bury that video," it would disappear faster than Paris Hilton's movies.

"Uh—" Gillian began, but I didn't stick around to listen. I took the marble stairs down to the common room three at a time. We were a couple. He would do something to help. I wasn't sure what, but at the very least, a show of solidarity would go a long way.

I tried to slow down on the way into the common room, but

the sight of Callum next to the couch wiped away everything but the need—the compulsion, even—to be in his arms. Protected. Soothed. Told that everything would be all right.

I fit myself against him, wound my arms around his waist, and waited for the comfort of his arms to slip around me.

And waited.

Finally I looked up, into his face. Those eyes held a frown, and the sweet grin I'd expected was a thin line.

"Uh, do you mind?" he said.

I didn't get it. "Mind?"

"I'm with my friends, Lissa."

Yeah, I saw that. What did it have to do with anything?

"She's still hot for ya, bro," Todd said with a nudge-nudge-wink-wink grin. "After last night, you must have stamina."

Callum told him where to shove it, and took me out into the hall by the arm like a little kid.

The crash between expectation and reality still had me stunned and confused. "Callum?"

"In case you missed the memo, Lissa, we are done. Don't tackle me in front of my friends. It makes me look lame and you look desperate."

"What?" I whispered. *Not keeping up here. Not keeping up at all.*

"I mean, you are one needy chick, but I can handle that. Most days. But after I told you twenty times that I like to keep my private life private, you still went ahead and did it. What was it, some kind of joke? Or a souvenir for you to watch whenever you want?"

"Did what?"

He rolled his eyes and took a deep breath, as if he was a parent at the end of his rope and I was a stupid two-year-old. "Hello? The video?"

"You saw it."

"Of course I saw it. The entire world saw it. It'll be on YouTube next. But that probably doesn't bother you, since all you care about is yourself."

"I didn't have anything to do with it. We were set up." Was that me whining, almost in tears?

Had I really thought it couldn't get worse?

"Sure, we were. You got me in a room and videotaped us! Who set up who?"

"Vanessa," I whispered. And then a thought hit me with all the force of truth. "She hates me because she wants you for herself."

He swore, something I'd never heard him do before. "That is the lamest, sorriest—" He took a breath, then said very slowly and deliberately, "Vanessa is my friend. You're not going to pin this on her. She is also a hundred miles away. About where I wish you were."

My lips trembled, and tears flooded my eyes. "Callum, please let me—" I whispered, but he cut me off.

"Don't talk to me anymore. I can't deal."

And he turned and left me. Alone. With the laughter of everyone in the common room ringing in my ears.

I don't know how long I stood there. Probably only a minute or two, but it seemed like hours. Then a couple of freshmen walked by and elbowed each other, and exchanged the kind of grin that made me feel like I was covered in slime.

I speed-walked down the hall, through another corridor, into the deserted classroom wing.

Aha. The French classroom. No one would come in there voluntarily.

I didn't want to go back to my room, where Gillian and Carly were probably waiting and wondering what on earth was going on downstairs. They were my friends, but what I needed really bad right now was the kind of friend who'd known me for years and who liked me anyway, in spite of my mistakes.

I needed Kaz.

I pulled my iPhone out of my pocket and scrolled to Kaz's name at lightspeed.

"This is Kaz Griffin. You know the drill."

I disconnected and tried again. Four more endless rings.

"This is—"

Arghh. I called his house and his dad picked up. "Hi, Mr. Griffin. It's Lissa."

"Hey, Lissa. How's it going in the big fog?"

"It's okay. Today could have been better. Is Kaz home? He's not answering his cell."

"As a matter of fact, the big galoot deserted me just when I needed him to crew. He took off for the weekend."

Took off? Kaz never took off. He hung out with us, or else he holed up in his bright, sunny loft and drew scary graphic novels about spiritual warfare that someday, some editor would get a clue and buy.

"Do you know where he went?" Like it would make a difference. My mouth was on autopilot while my brain replayed today's horrors over and over.

"I can't say, Lissa. I'm sorry. Can I take a message?"

Weren't parents supposed to know where their kids were? Did Kaz know what a clueless dad he had? "If he checks in, just ask him to call me."

"I will. Keep on rockin' in the free world."

"Right. Well, bye, Mr. G."

I hung up and sat, hands drooping hopelessly between my knees, under a poster that showed how to conjugate a dozen irregular verbs.

How was it possible that my life could go from all shiny and golden to slimy and hopeless in a single day? All I'd wanted was to show Callum how much I cared about him. That's all. How come everyone else on the planet got to make out like minxes with their boyfriends, and I got ground into the dirt like a bug under a boot heel?

And then, as though someone had hit a remote, my memory recycled a bit of audio. "All bets are off when we deliberately book a room and walk into it," Gillian said. And then Kaz, right on top of it: "If this were right, would we even be talking about broken rules and broken promises?"

Kaz had a chameleon character in his novel—one who shape-shifted whenever he needed to, but who was essentially a lizard underneath. He was one of the most successful agents of evil, because you never knew if you were talking to a friend or this character wearing the friend's face. Vanessa had assured me there were ways to have fun and still stay pure—technically. But that was like saying I could be a technical Christian, wasn't it? I might follow the letter of the law, but as soon as I started doing that, the Spirit leached right out of it and I was stuck with the consequences.

Now *I figure this out.*

Now, when it was hours too late and the consequences were way too hard to face, let alone live through.

Elbows on my knees, I buried my face in my hands. Whether I deserved to ask or not, I had no place else to go.

I'm sorry, Lord. You sent me Gillian and Kaz when I needed them. Your timing was perfect. But I ignored them and listened to the chameleon instead. All I can do is drag my sorry self in front of You again and ask You one more time to forgive me.

And I know it's a stretch, but if there's some way You can help me get through the rest of today, tonight, and maybe even next week, I'll be a different person. I'll listen, Lord. I need to stay close to You so You can help me discern who's a chameleon and who's real. And so You won't have to reach so far to give me a shake and tell me to change what I'm doing.

Help me, Father. I really need You. Amen.

Sitting there in that deserted classroom, with no sound except the hum of the air conditioner and my own sniffly, running nose, I finally felt as if I'd done the right thing.

I know. One out of ten ain't bad.

chapter 26

"DADDY, I NEED HELP."

My father leaned on my wardrobe door and surveyed Gillian's and my room. Mom's flight hadn't landed yet, but when it did, she'd come straight here and change for the ball. Only my mother could pack a designer evening gown in a carry-on, whip into the nearest ladies' room, and come out looking fabulous.

"I figured you might. I heard your mom's best girl fell through."

So she'd told him. But had he heard from Ms. Curzon yet? I shivered and decided not to bring it up. Better not ruin their day until I had to. "Yes. Rumor has it that I was supposed to have a Plan B, but I don't."

"And rumor also has it that George is on location and a ball player I know has a gig of his own tonight."

"You checked?"

"Yeah. I'm kinda used to playing second fiddle, so I thought I'd check the rest of the fiddles while I was at it."

Uh-oh. I didn't like the sound of this. My father was not the poor-me type. "Daddy, is everything okay?"

"Oh, sure. Don't mind me—I'm just twelve hours short on

sleep. Been busy up at the Ranch. We're probably going to start shooting in December. How do you feel about Scotland?"

"How do I feel about it? It's wet and cold and most of it's above the Arctic Circle."

"Gosh." He glanced admiringly at the architecture. "You really are getting an education in this place, aren't you?"

"Why?"

"Oh, I was just wondering if you wanted to spend Christmas with me in Edinburgh, is all."

Christmas. Only seventy-two shopping days away. On a whole different continent. Where I'd need a parka, but who cared?

"That could be doable, Dad. I wouldn't mind getting away from here for the holidays." *Focus.* "But that still leaves me with no host." And then I had it. "Unless *you* did it."

"Me? Did what? Went to Scotland?"

"No. You can be my celebrity host. Every kid in school saw *Crossing Blades.* They all know who directed it. You're as good as a movie star any day."

"Probably more articulate, too."

"So you'll do it?"

"I had to get my tux out of mothballs. I may as well make it worth my while."

I let out a long sigh and hugged him. "I know you hate it in front of cameras, but thanks for being here for me."

"If I let you down, at least you'd know where to send the hit men. What does this entail, exactly?"

"We have a script for you. All you have to do is read it off the TelePrompTer. Just like at the Oscars." I smiled at him, happy that one thing—just one—had gone right on The Day from You-Know-Where.

"Speaking of performances," he said, though we hadn't been, "I got an interesting call from your headmistress as I was driving over here."

Oh, no. My single little ray of light winked out.

"I can explain."

"I hope so," Dad said mildly. "Smuggling boys into your room?"

"Not my room. Another girl's. But, yeah. Smuggling about covers it."

"And he was what, helping you install a stereo system?"

I sighed. "No, Dad. We wanted some privacy."

"Oh." Clearly my dad has been in denial about the fact that I'm sixteen, despite all the evidence.

"And did it have the desired result?"

I took a deep breath. "The result wound up on the school server. On all the monitors in every classroom. Probably, by now, on YouTube. It was a beautiful evening with my boyf—my ex-boyfriend—that was digitally manipulated from webcam footage, and now the whole school is laughing at me."

I waited for him to say something. "I told you so," maybe. Or "How dumb can you be, Lissa?" Or even, "Next time you visit, you're grounded."

Dad scrubbed a hand over his hair, making the cowlick stand up straight. Then he looked at me, and his eyes held all the dis-appointment I'd been dreading. And they held something else. "I don't suppose dismemberment would be an acceptable addition to tonight's program?"

"I'd rather you did it in private, Dad. I've had enough humiliation to do me for the next decade."

"I didn't mean you."

Dad pulled me roughly into his arms. His face felt hot, and his arms moved in jerks, as if he was struggling for control. I pulled back a little to look, and there they were.

Tears in my dad's eyes. For me.

The dam broke then. I won't tell you how long we stood there, or who comforted who. But by the time Gillian slipped into the room, I felt as though a tsunami had gone over me, and my little personal beach was washed clean.

So was my face. I detoured into the bathroom to splash cold water on it and try to get a grip. When I came out, Gillian's appearance had helped Dad rein in his emotions, too.

"This isn't finished," he said. "Is there something we can do?"

"I can't prove a thing." I was getting to the point where I didn't want to talk about it anymore. Moving on was the plan. Moving out would be better. "Vanessa was a hundred miles away with her boyfriend. Callum seems to think I'm the one behind it. Like I want the whole school thinking I'm some kind of skank."

"Lissa," Dad said in a muffled tone.

"I want out of here, Dad. I want to go back to Santa Barbara."

He pulled a tissue out of the box on Gillian's dresser and blew his nose. "Not happening, baby. We all agreed that we'd live here for two years."

"Yeah, but we didn't count on me being so stupid and Vanessa being . . . Vanessa. I was happy in Santa Barbara. If I go this week, I won't miss very much school. The term's got seven weeks to go."

"You can't just run away," Gillian said.

"She's right," Dad said. "Running away doesn't solve a thing. Not when e-mail can beat you to wherever you're going."

I had a sudden horrific vision of that video making the rounds of Pacific High, and actually had to sit down. I thought it was bad now, when only a handful of people knew me. What if all my friends saw it? If I went back and the news broke, I'd go from A-list to walk-on in less time than it took to say "Ooh!"

"Come on, Lissa." Gillian slipped an arm around my shoulders and squeezed. "It's nearly time to get dressed."

I stared at her. Was she crazed? "I'm not going to the stupid ball."

"Yes, you are. You're going with Carly and me."

And face two hundred students, the trustees, the parents, and San Francisco's philanthropists and media? I shook my head. "Not a chance. You can show Dad down to the assembly hall."

"You're on the committee. The celebrity speaker is your job."

"I'm delegating it to you."

Gillian rocked back on her heels, crossed her arms, and stuck out a hip. "I refuse."

"Then I'll ask—" Who? Vanessa? DeLayne? Dani? Not happening. "Carly."

"Nuh-uh. Major stage fright. Looks like you're down to one. You."

I glared at her, then at Dad. Why wasn't he jumping in to take my side? "What are you trying to do to me? Aren't things bad enough?"

She leaned in and gave me the I'm-gonna-drill-Genetics-into-you-if-it's-the-last-thing-I-do stare. The one that had jump-started my brain and netted me a blessed C+ on that horrific project. "If you back down now, things will get infinitely worse. You're going to put that dress on, go out there, and face them down with your best blond-princess impression. You're going to walk to that microphone and introduce your father, and you're going to do it with style. And after that, you're going to stick to Ms. Curzon like white on rice."

If I did that, no one would have the guts to say anything. They'd laugh at their tables and probably make dirty jokes at my expense, but I wouldn't hear it. I'd be there in the spotlight but—

I gasped. The spotlight. "The committee dance! I don't have a partner. I can't do it."

"I'll dance with you, L-squared," Dad offered.

Now, don't get me wrong, I love my dad and he knows it, but there was no way on this green earth that I was going to get out there in that spotlight with my father.

"We'll jump off that bridge when we get to it." Gillian took me by the shoulders and pushed me toward the bathroom. "Makeup. Hair. This is supposed to be the fun part. Carly's coming back with her dress and we're going to have a party getting ready."

My dad grinned and kissed me. "Guess that's my cue to exit stage right. I'll find my way to the assembly hall and save you three beautiful girls a seat."

"And one for Carly's dad, please," Gillian said.

Dad nodded and smiled at me one last time as he left.

I took a deep breath and faced Gillian, who could probably take on an army of demons armed only with a toothpick and a length of dental floss. "I don't deserve you."

She blew me a raspberry. "What else are friends for?"

"Oh, I dunno. Being sworn at, dumped, not listened to, and generally abandoned."

"I knew you'd see the light eventually. I just didn't expect it to be quite so . . . public."

"Me either. Friends forever?"

She leaned in for a hug. "Now, get in there and make yourself pretty for the party."

For once, I did as she suggested. If I'd learned nothing else, it was that once Gillian gave her friendship, it was for good.

And I mean that in every sense of the word.

chapter 27

N A DRESS like this, even Ugly Betty could pull off a blond-princess impression. The hidden bones in the bodice forced my chest out and my shoulders back, so that even Mrs. Mirkova, the social dance teacher Kaz and I had had when we were kids, couldn't have complained about my posture.

"Walk in like you own the place."

I stared at Carly as we crossed the lawn to the building that housed the assembly hall and the dramatic arts classrooms. The big double doors, flanked by Italian cypresses imported for the occasion and surmounted by a twenty-foot banner welcoming the benefactors to campus, were just ahead. To my knowledge, Carly was shy and insecure and prone to running errands for people who didn't appreciate it. Where had she learned to own a room?

Gillian, between the two of us, took our hands in a brief grip as we walked up. "It's all about us," she said. "Not the video, not what people think or say. It's all about us and God, together. And don't forget, we've got an army of angels at our backs."

It didn't have to be us. It could have just been me out there for everyone to stare at, with Gillian and Carly floating in the background and God out even further, a vengeful presence saying, "You had this coming, girlfriend."

But instead, I felt like a conquering army—or at least, part of something bigger than me, with love and courage and friendship trickling in to blot out the shame. Was it proof that God had forgiven me? I wasn't sure, but one thing I knew: This feeling was something I could count on to get me through the next couple of hours.

Or maybe I was overdramatizing just to get myself through that door.

We swept past the greeters and into the assembly hall. Vanessa and her army of decorators had gone all out, with sweeping swags of gold cloth, blue and gold banners hanging from the ceiling, potted trees festooned in fairy lights, and blue damask napkins folded between place settings of gold at every round table.

Dad waved at us from a table at the front, where he was sitting with my mom and a slender guy about the same age.

"Papa!" The man got up and Carly ran into his arms, her skirt making a froufrou of motion around her ankles.

"I'm sorry I'm late," he said. "The flight from Narita was delayed."

"You're in time for the fun, and that's what matters. Papa, these are my friends, Gillian Chang and Lissa Mansfield."

"I'm very happy to meet your friends, *mi hija*," Mr. Aragon said fondly. "You look lovely, ladies."

"*Gracias,*" I said. "It's all thanks to Carly. She took us to the garment district and saved us from ourselves."

I hugged Mom, who, as predicted, looked completely fabulous in Vera Wang, and introduced her to Carly.

A sudden rise in the noise level off to the right was my only warning when Vanessa appeared, fuming and gorgeous in a black strapless Miu Miu minidress. Very, very mini.

"There you are," she said, as though I'd been leading her on a merry chase all evening. "Who have you got?"

"Sorry?" For what? A dance partner? A celebrity speaker?

"For your Plan B." Man, if she didn't ease up on the orthodontia, she was going to crack a molar.

"Oh, that." I gave her a big smile. "You look great, Vanessa. Have you met my parents, Gabe Mansfield and Patricia Sutter? And Carly's father, Mr. Aragon?"

She shook hands with barely concealed impatience before I took pity on her. No matter what she'd done to me, the success of this event was on her shoulders. I didn't envy her that one bit. We'd deal with what lay between us after it was all over.

"My father has agreed to do the welcome," I told her. "I think everyone in the room knows his name. Now they'll have a face to put with it."

Since he was standing right there, Vanessa could do nothing but put on a public smile and accept reality as gracefully as possible. No matter what else she might be, she wasn't a fool.

Not like some of us, sometimes. Sigh.

She wrote his name in the slender planner that fit in her evening bag, and glanced at me. "So. Who can I put down as your partner for the committee dance?"

Ow. Way to slide the blade between the ribs, Vanessa.

"Isn't it in the program?"

"No, of course not. But the—your dad will announce each of the committee members and their partners as they take the floor."

And she stood there waiting for me to reply, malice sparkling in her eyes.

"She'll get back to you on that," Gillian said from beside me. "She's got a couple of options."

I did?

"She does?" Vanessa's tone told me she saw right through that one. "Be sure to let me know before showtime, won't you?"

Then she turned on her Manolo heel and left.

We sat at the table, and a college-aged guy in a tux took our drink orders.

"Who, exactly, are my options?" I murmured to Gillian on my right. Mom and Dad sat on my left, then Carly, then her dad. "Or maybe I should say *what* are my options? As far as I can see, I've got two—making a run for the bathroom, or dancing with Dad."

"Don't panic," she whispered back. "It'll all work out. Hey, check out DeLayne Geary. I'll bet you a semester of room cleaning that that dress came from the same designer as Carly's."

Clothes-watching, my favorite spectator sport, was for once not enough to make the heavy clump of nerves in my stomach go away, or to keep my knees from rattling together. Thank goodness for the filmy layers of silk chiffon.

I managed to choke my salad down with the help of a lot of ice water. But the entrée—medallions of pork and eggplant with a white wine pepper sauce—was more than I could take. Luckily Dad had no such difficulties, and soon my plate was as clean as his.

"Your dresses are gorgeous, girls," my mother said. "Lissa, I would never have put you in that, but I have to say, it's a terrific choice."

"You've got to check out the designer, Mom. I got her card for you. She's from Hungary, and her brother worked on one of Dad's films."

"I absolutely will. The Babies of Somalia benefit is almost on us and I could use something unusual. What about Gillian's? Where'd it come from?"

Get my mom started on clothes and new designers, and she's good for at least two courses. Dessert came, and then it was time for the speeches. Suddenly I lost interest in my cheesecake. And that takes a major crisis, let me tell you.

I won't go into all the speeches and rich people thanking each other, or you'll be as bored as I was, minus the stomach cramps and the sense that since the day wasn't over, it must hold one final disaster.

After all the suits, Curzon introduced Vanessa, who had her moment in the sun as the organizer of the event. And then she looked at our table.

Cue disaster.

"Unfortunately," she said into the mike with a beautiful smile, "our advertised celebrity guest was unable to be with us due to a family emergency. However, I'm very happy to introduce one of our school's own parents, who agreed to step in at the eleventh hour. Ladies and gentlemen, Mr. Gabriel Mansfield, director of *Crossing Blades*."

Huge applause—way more than Vanessa got. Dad walked up to the podium and read the welcome off the TelePrompTer as if he'd written it himself. I'd have felt proud of him if I hadn't been trying not to throw up. Just a few more seconds . . .

And there it was. "Now, for the first dance, I'd like to introduce the members of the committee who worked so hard to make Benefactors' Day such a golden success." The band swung into a tune I vaguely recognized from swing-dance class, years ago. Kaz would know what it was. His musical vocab was way bigger than mine. I gulped and tried to hold it together as Dad called Vanessa's name along with Brett Loyola's.

Carly slid down in her chair about two inches, her gaze riveted to the dance floor, where Vanessa and Brett whirled and swung in the spotlight.

"DeLayne Geary, publicity and public relations, partnered by Michael Thomas." The audience applauded politely. "Christina Powell, catering, partnered by Todd Runyon."

"Ew," Gillian said in my ear.

"Lissa Mansfield—"

I gasped and stood up, feeling like a deer in the headlights.

Who? Who would I ask? Would Carly's dad dance with me? How could I let Dad know to call his name? *Oh no oh no . . .*

"—relations, partnered by Charles Canfield Griffin."

Charles what? Who?

I swayed, certain I was about to faint.

And then the spotlight swung onto a tall guy in a black morning coat, with a spotless white shirt and black tie. And that was where formality ended.

Shaggy surfer hair.

Brown eyes, smiling under his bangs.

A dimple big enough to put a finger in.

Kaz took my ice-cold, limp hand, and Gillian gave me an unobtrusive push in the small of my back. The spotlight blinded me, but I trusted Kaz as he guided me out onto the floor and whirled me into a swing pattern we'd learned years ago. My dress floated out and the silver tracery caught the light, just the way I'd imagined it. It probably caught the tears in my eyes, too.

"Surprise," he whispered, pulling me into a dance hold and whirling me out again. "Nice dress."

"Kaz." I couldn't get anything else out. I was too busy gazing pathetically into his face, hoping he wasn't a hologram, about to vanish in a puff of electrons. "Your dad said you were gone for the weekend."

"I am. Here." He turned me into a sweetheart hold and passed me in front of him, then back. "I swore him to secrecy in case you called. I drove all day. Made it here in the nick of time."

"But how did—how—?"

"Your friend Gillian called me. Damsels in distress—can't resist 'em."

"Bless her," I breathed, back in a waltz hold again. "And bless you. I don't know what I would have done if you hadn't—if you weren't—"

"But I'm here," he said. I felt the warmth of his hand on my back, guiding me in and out of the steps. "Gillian and your other friends are here. God's here. We're all in this together, and we're not leaving."

I felt the truth of it, as though someone had struck a tuning fork deep inside. No matter what I had to face on Monday, or next week, or next year . . . no matter how often I made mistakes . . . I had my friends. I had my family. And most important of all, I had the Lord behind me. It was all about us, after all.

Bring it on, Spencer Academy.

And we'll see who wins.

about the author

Shelley Adina wrote her first teen novel when she was thirteen. It was rejected by the literary publisher to whom she sent it, but he did say she knew how to tell a story. That was enough to keep her going through the rest of her adolescence, a career, a move to another country, a B.A. in Literature, an M.A. in Writing Popular Fiction, and countless manuscript pages.

Shelley is a world traveler and pop culture junkie with an incurable addiction to designer handbags. She knows the value of a relationship with a gracious God and loving Christian friends, and she loves writing about fun and faith—with a side of glamour. Between books, Shelley loves traveling, listening to and making music, and watching all kinds of movies.

IF YOU LIKED

it's all about us,

check out the second book in the series:

the fruit of my lipstick

available this August!

Turn the page for a sneak peek. . . .

chapter 1

TOP FIVE CLUES that He's the One:

1. He's smart, which is why he's dating you and not the
   queen of the snob mob.
2. He knows he's hot, but he thinks you're hotter.
3. He'd rather listen to you than himself.
4. You're in on his jokes—not the butt of them.
5. He always gives you the last cookie in the box.

THE NEW YEAR . . . when a young girl's heart turns to new
beginnings, weight loss, and a new term of *chemistry*!

Whew! Got that little squee out of my system. But you may
as well know right now that science and music are what I do,
and they tend to come up a lot in conversation. Sometimes my
friends think this is good, like when I'm helping them cram for
an exam. Sometimes they just think I'm a geek. But that's okay.
My name is Gillian Frances Jiao-Lan Chang, and since Lissa was
brave enough to fall on her sword and spill what happened last
fall, I guess I can't do anything less.

I'm kidding about the sword. You know that, right?

Term was set to start on the first Wednesday in January, so I flew into SFO nonstop from JFK on Monday. I thought I packed pretty efficiently, but I still exceeded the weight limit by fifty pounds. It took some doing to get me and my bags into the limo, let me tell you. But I'd found last term that I couldn't live without certain things, so they came with me. Like my sheet music and some more of my books. And warmer clothes.

You say *California* and everyone thinks *L.A.* The reality of San Francisco in the winter is that it's cold, whether the sun is shining or the fog is stealing in through the Golden Gate and blanketing the bay. A perfect excuse for a trip to Barney's to get Vera Wang's tulip-hem black wool coat, right?

I thought so, too.

Dorm sweet dorm. I staggered through the door of the room I share with Lissa Mansfield. It's up to us to get our stuff into our rooms, so here's where it pays to be on the rowing team, I guess. Biceps are good for hauling fifty-pound Louis Vuittons up marble staircases. But I am *so* not the athletic type. I leave that to John, the youngest of my three older brothers. He's been into gymnastics since he was, like, four, and he's training hard to make the U.S. Olympics team. I haven't seen him since I was fourteen—he trains with a coach out in Arizona.

My oldest brother, Richard, is twenty-six and works for my dad at the bank, and my second-oldest, Darren—the one I'm closest to—is graduating next spring from Harvard, going straight into medical school after that.

Yeah, we're a family of overachievers. Don't hate me, okay?

I heard a thump in the hall outside, and got the door open just in time to come face-to-face with a huge piece of striped fiberglass with three fins.

I stood aside to let Lissa into the room with her surfboard. She was practically bowed at the knees with the weight of the duffel slung over her shoulder, and another duffel with a big O'Neill logo waited outside. I grabbed it and swung it onto her bed.

"Welcome back, girlfriend!"

She stood the board against the wall, let the duffel drop to the floor with a thud that probably shook the chandelier in the room below us, and pulled me into a hug.

"I am so glad to see you!" Her perfect Nordic face had lit up with happiness. "How was your Christmas—the parts you didn't tell me about on e-mail?"

"The usual. Too many family parties. Mom and Nai-Nai made way too much food, two of my brothers fought over the remote like they were ten years old, my dad and oldest brother bailed to go back to work early, and oh, Nai-Nai wanted to know at least twice a day why I didn't have a boyfriend." I considered the chaos we'd just made of our pristine room. "The typical Chang holiday. What about you? Did Scotland improve after the first couple of days?"

"It was fre-e-e-e-zing." She slipped off her coat and tam. "And I don't just mean rainy freezing. I mean sleet and icicles freezing. The first time I wore my high-heeled Louboutin boots I nearly broke my ankle. As it was, I landed flat on my butt in the middle of the Royal Mile. Totally embarrassing."

"What's a Royal Mile? Princesses by the square foot?"

"This big broad avenue that goes through the old part of town toward the queen's castle. Good shopping. Restaurants. Tourists. Ice." She unzipped the duffel and began pulling things out of it. "Dad was away a lot at the locations for this movie. Sometimes I went with him, and sometimes I hung out with this really adorable guy who was supposed to be somebody's production assistant but who wound up being my guide the whole time."

"It's a tough job, but someone's gotta do it."

"I made it worth his while." She flashed me a wicked grin, but behind it I saw something else. Pain, and memory. "So." She spread her hands. "What's new around here?"

I shrugged. "I just walked in myself a few minutes ago. You probably passed the limo leaving. But if what you really want to know is whether the webcam incident is over and done with, I don't know yet."

She turned away, but not before I saw her flush pink and then blink really fast, like her contacts had just been flooded. "Let's hope so."

"You made it through last term." I tried to be encouraging. "What doesn't kill you makes you stronger, right?"

"It made one thing stronger." She pulled a cashmere scarf out of the duffel and stroked it as though it were a kitten. "I never prayed so hard in my life. Especially during finals week, remember? When those two idiots seriously thought they could force me into that storage closet and get away with it?"

"Before we left, I heard the short one was going to be in a cast for six weeks." I grinned at her. Fact of the day: Surfers are pretty good athletes. Don't mess with them. "Maybe it should be 'What doesn't kill you makes your relationship with God stronger.'"

"That I'll agree with. Do you know if Carly's here yet?"

"Her dad was driving her up in time for supper, so she should be calling any second."

Sure enough, within a few minutes someone knocked. "That's gotta be her." I jumped for the door and swung it open.

"Hey, *chicas!*" Carly hugged me and then Lissa. "Did you miss me?"

"Like chips miss guacamole." Lissa grinned at her. "Good break?"

She grimaced, her soft brown eyes a little sad. Clearly Christmas break isn't what it's cracked up to be in *anybody's* world.

"Dad had to go straighten out some computer chip thing in Singapore, so Antony and I got shipped off to Veracruz. It was great to see my mom and the grandparents, but you know . . ." Her voice trailed away.

"What?" I asked. "Did you have a fight?" This is what happens at our house.

"No." She sighed, then lifted her head to look at both of us. "I think my mom has a boyfriend."

"Ewww," Lissa and I said together, with identical grimaces.

"I always kind of hoped my mom and dad would figure it out, you know? And get back together. But it looks like that's not going to happen."

I hugged her again. "I'm sorry, Carly. That stinks."

"Yeah." She straightened up, and my arm slid from her shoulders. "So, enough about me. What about you guys?"

With a quick recap, we put her in the picture. "So do you have something going with this Scottish guy?" Carly asked Lissa.

Lissa shook her head, a curtain of blond hair falling to partially hide her face. A trick I've never quite been able to master—even though my hair hangs past my shoulders. But it's so thick and coarse it never does what I want on the best of days. It has to be beaten into submission by a professional.

"I think I liked his accent most of all," she said. "I could just sit there and listen to him talk all day. In fact, I did. What he doesn't know about murders and wars and Edinburgh Castle and Lord This and Earl That would probably fit in my lip gloss tube."

I contrasted walking the cold streets of Edinburgh listening to some guy drone on about history with fighting with my brothers. Do we girls know how to have fun, or what? "Better you than me."

"I'd have loved it," Carly said. "Can you imagine walking through a castle with your own private tour guide? Especially if he's cute. It doesn't get better than that."

"Um, okay." Lissa gave her a sideways glance. "Miss A-plus in History."

"Really?" I had A-pluses in AP Chem and Math, but with anything less I wouldn't have been able to face my father at

Christmas. As it was, he had a fit over my B in History, and the only reason I had an A-minus in English was because of a certain person with the initials L.M."

Carly shrugged. "I like history. I like knowing what happened in places, and who it happened to, and what they were wearing. Not that I've ever been anywhere very much, except Texas and Mexico."

"You'd definitely have liked Alasdair, then," Lissa said. "He knows all about what happened to who. But the worst was having to go for tea at some freezing old stone castle that Dad was using for a set. I thought I'd lose my toes from frostbite."

"Somebody lives in the castle?" Carly looked fascinated. "Who?"

"Some earl." Lissa looked into the distance as she flipped through the PDA in her head. Then she blinked. "The Earl and Countess of Strathcairn."

"Cool!"

"Very. At least forty degrees. He said he had a daughter about our age but I never met her. She heard we were coming and took off on her horse."

"*Mo guai nuer,*" I said. "Rude much?"

Lissa shrugged. "Alasdair knew the family. He said Lady Lindsay does what she wants, and clearly she didn't want to meet us. Not that I care. I was too busy having hypothermia. I've never been so glad to see the inside of a hotel room in my life. I'd have put my feet in my mug of tea if I could have."

"Well, cold or not, I still think it's cool that you met an earl," Carly said. "And I can't wait to see your dad's movie."

"Filming starts in February, so Dad won't be around much. But Mom's big charity gig for the Babies of Somalia went off just before Christmas and was a huge success, so she'll be around a bit more." She paused. "Until she finds something else to get involved in."

"Did you meet Angelina?" I asked. Lissa's life fascinated me. To her, movie stars are her dad's coworkers, like the finance guys at the bank are my dad's coworkers. But Dad doesn't work with people who look like Orlando and Angelina, that's for sure.

"Yes, I met her. She apologized for flaking on me for the Benefactors' Day ball. Not that I blame her. It all turned out okay in the end."

"Except for your career as Vanessa Talbot's BFF."

Lissa snorted. "Yeah. Except that."

None of us mentioned what else had crashed and burned in flames after the infamous webcam incident—her relationship with the most popular guy in school, Callum McCloud. I had a feeling that was a scab we just didn't need to pick at.

"You don't need Vanessa Talbot," Carly said firmly. "You have us."

We exchanged a grin. "She's right," I said. "This term, it's totally all about us."

"Thank goodness for that," she said. "Come on. Let's go eat. I'm starving."

RStapleton	I heard from a mutual friend that you take care of people at midterm time.
Source10	What friend?
RStapleton	Loyola.
Source10	Been known to happen.
RStapleton	How much?
Source10	1K. Math, sciences, geography only.
RStapleton	I hate numbers.
Source10	IM me the day before to confirm.
RStapleton	OK. Who are you?
RStapleton	You there?

By noon the next day, I'd hustled down to the student print shop in the basement and printed the notices I'd laid out on my

Mac. I tacked them on the bulletin boards in the common rooms and classroom corridors on all four floors.

*Christian Prayer Circle every Tuesday night
7:00 p.m., Room 216
Bring your Bible and a friend!*

"Nice work," Lissa told me when I found her and Carly in the dining room. "Love the salmon pink paper. But school hasn't officially started yet. We probably won't get a very good turnout if the first one's tonight."

"Maybe not." I bit into a succulent California roll and savored the tart, thin seaweed wrapper around the rice, avocado, and shrimp. I had to hand it to Dining Services. Their food is amazing. "But even if it's just the three of us, I can't think of a better way to start off the term, can you?"

Instead of replying, the color faded from her face and she concentrated on her square ceramic plate of sushi as though it were her last meal. Carly swallowed a bite of makizushi with an audible gulp as it went down whole. Slowly, casually, I reached for the pepper shaker and glanced over my shoulder.

"If it isn't the holy trinity," Vanessa drawled, plastered against Brett Loyola's arm and standing so close behind us neither Carly nor I could move. "Going to multiply the rice and fish for us?"

"Nice to see you, too, Vanessa," Lissa said coolly. "Been reading your Bible, I see."

"Hi, Brett," Carly managed, her voice about six notes higher than usual.

He looked at her, puzzled, as if he'd seen her before somewhere but couldn't place where, and gave her a vague smile. "Hey."

I rolled my eyes. Like we hadn't spent an entire term in History together. Like Carly didn't light up like a Christmas tree every time she passed a paper to him or maneuvered her way into a study group that had him in it. Honestly. I don't know how that guy got past the entrance requirements.

Oh, wait. Silly me. Daddy probably made a nice big donation to the athletics department, and they waved Brett through Admissions with a grateful smile.

"Have any of you seen Callum?" Vanessa inquired sweetly. "I'm dying to see him. I hear he spent Christmas skiing at their place in Vail with his sisters and his new girlfriend. No parents."

"He's a day student." I glanced at Lissa to see how she was taking this, but she'd leaned over to the table behind her to snag a bunch of napkins. "Why would he be eating here?"

"To see all his friends, of course. I guess that's why *you* haven't seen him."

"Neither have you, if you're asking where he is." Poor Vanessa. I hope she's never on a debating team. It could get humiliating.

But what she lacked in logic she made up for in venom. She ignored me and gushed, "I love your outfit, Lissa. I'm sure Callum would, too. That is, if he were still speaking to you."

I barely restrained myself from giving Vanessa an elbow in the stomach. But Lissa had come a long way since her ugly breakup with a guy who didn't deserve her. Vanessa had no idea who she was dealing with. Lissa with an army of angels at her back was a scary thing.

She pinned Vanessa with a stare as cold as fresh snow.

"You mean you haven't told him yet that *you* made that video?" She shook her head. "Naughty Vanessa, lying to your friends like that." A big smile and a meaningful glance at Brett. "But then, they're probably used to it."

Vanessa opened her mouth to say something scathing, when a tall, lanky guy elbowed past her to put his sushi dishes on the table next to mine. Six feet of sheer brilliance, with blue eyes and brown hair cropped short so he doesn't have to deal with it. A mind so sharp he put even the overachievers here in the shade—but in spite of that, a guy who'd started coming to prayer circle last term.

Who could fluster me with a look, and wipe my brain completely blank with just a smile.

Lucas Hayes.

"Hey, Vanessa, Brett."

My jaw sagged in surprise, and I quickly snapped it shut on my mouthful of rice, hoping he hadn't seen. Since when was the king of the science geeks on speaking terms with the popular crowd?

To add to the astonishment, the two of them stepped back, as if to give him some space. "Yo, Einstein." Brett grinned and they shook hands.

"Hi, Lucas." Vanessa glanced from him to me to our dishes sitting next to each other. "I didn't know you were friends with these people."

He shrugged. "There's a lot you don't know about me."

"That could change. Why don't you come and sit with us?" she asked. Brett looked longingly at the sushi bar and tugged on her arm. She ignored him. "We're much more fun. We don't sing hymns and save souls."

"So I've heard. Did you make it into Trig?"

"Of course." She tossed her gleaming sheet of hair over one shoulder. "Thanks to you."

I couldn't keep quiet another second. "You *tutored* her?" I asked him, trying not to squeak.

He picked up a piece of California roll and popped it in his mouth, nodding. "All last term." He glanced at Vanessa. "Contrary to popular opinion, she isn't all looks."

Oh, gack, way TMI. Vanessa smiled as though she'd won this and all other possible arguments now and in the future, world without end, amen. "Come on, Lucas. Hold our table for us while Brett and I get our food. I want to talk to you about something anyway."

He shrugged and picked up his dishes while she and Brett swanned away. "See you at prayer circle," he said to me. "I saw the signs. Same time and place, right?"

I could only nod as he headed for the table in the middle of the big window looking out on the quad. The one no one else dared to sit at, in case they risked the derision and social disaster that would follow.

The empty seat on my right seemed even emptier. How could he do that? How could he just dump us and then say he'd see us at prayer circle? Shouldn't he want to eat with the people he prayed with?

"It's okay, Gillian," Carly whispered. "At least he's coming."

"And Vanessa isn't," Lissa put in with satisfaction.

"I'm not so sure I want him to, now," I said. I looked at my sushi and my stomach sort of lurched. Ugh. I pushed it away.

And here I'd been feeling so superior to Carly and her unrequited yen for Brett. I was just as bad, and this proved it. What else could explain this sick feeling in my middle?

Two hours later, while Lissa, Carly, and I shoved aside the canvases and whatnot that had accumulated in room 216 over Christmas break, making enough room for half a dozen people to sit, I'd almost talked myself into not caring whether Lucas came or not.

And then he stepped through the door and I realized my body was more honest than my brain—I sucked in a breath and my heart began to pound.

Oh, yeah. You so don't *care.*

Travis, who must have arrived during dinner, trickled in behind him, and then Shani Hanna, who moved with the confidence of an Arabian queen, arrived with a couple of sophomores I didn't know. Her hair, tinted bronze and caught up at the crown of her head, tumbled to her shoulders in corkscrew curls. I fingered my own arrow-straight mop that wouldn't hold a curl if you threatened it with death.

Okay, stop feeling sorry for yourself and pray for someone, would you? Enough is enough.

"Hey, everyone, thanks for coming," I said brightly, getting to my feet. "I'm Gillian Chang. Why don't the newbies introduce themselves, and then we'll get started?"

The sophomores told us their names, and I found out Travis's last name was Fanshaw. And the dots connected. Of course he'd been assigned as Lucas's roommate—he's like this Chemistry genius. If it weren't for Lucas, *he'd* be the king of the science geeks. Sometimes science people have a hard time reconciling scientific method with faith. If they were here at prayer circle, maybe Travis and Lucas were among the lucky few who figured science was a form of worship, of marveling at the amazement that is creation. I mean, if Lucas was one of those guys who got a kick out of arguing with the Earth Sciences prof, I wouldn't even be able to date him.

Not that there was any possibility of that.

As our prayers went up one by one, quietly from people like Lissa and brash and uncomfortably from people like Travis and the sophomores, I wished that dating was the kind of thing I could pray about.

But I don't think God has my social life on His to-do list.

AND IF YOU THINK

the fruit of my lipstick,

LOOKS GOOD,

take a look at the third book in the series:

be strong and curvaceous

available in January 2009!

Turn the page for a sneak peek. . . .

chapter 1

BE CAREFUL WHAT you wish for.

I used to think that was the dumbest saying ever. I mean, when you wish for something, by definition it's wonderful, right? Like buying a new dress for a party. Or snagging a roommate as cool as Gillian Chang or Lissa Mansfield. Or having a guy notice you after six months of being invisible. Before last term, of course I wanted those wishes to come true.

I should have been more careful.

Let me back up a little. My name is Carolina Isabella Aragon Velasquez . . . but that doesn't fit on school admission forms, so when I started first grade it got shortened up to Carolina Aragon—Carly to my friends. Up until I was a sophomore, I lived with my mom and dad, my older sister Alana and little brother Antony in a huge house in Monte Sereno, just south of Silicon Valley. The company my dad owned invented some kind of security software for stock exchanges and he and everyone who worked for him got rich.

Then came what Dad calls Black Thursday and the stock market crash and suddenly my mom was leaving him and going to live with her parents in Veracruz, Mexico, to be an artist and find herself. Alana finished college and moved to Austin, where we have lots of relatives. Antony and I stayed with Dad in a condo about the size of our old living room, and since Dad spends so much time on the road, where I've found myself since September is boarding school.

The spring term started in April, and as I got out of the limo Dad sends me back to Spencer Academy in every Sunday night—even though I'm perfectly capable of taking the train—I couldn't help but feel a little bubble of optimism deep inside. Call me corny, but the news that Vanessa Talbot and Brett Loyola had broken up just before spring break had made the last ten days the happiest I'd had since my parents split up. Even flying to Veracruz and being introduced to my mother's boyfriend hadn't put a dent in it.

Ugh. Okay, I lied. *So* not going there.

Thinking about Brett now. Dark, romantic eyes. Curly dark hair, cut short because he's the captain of the rowing team. Broad shoulders. Fabulous clothes he wears as if he doesn't care where he got them.

Oh, yeah. Much better.

Lost in happy plans for how I'd finally get his attention (I was signing up to be a chem tutor first thing because let's face it, he needs me), I pushed open the door to my room and staggered in with my duffel bags.

My hands loosened and I dropped everything with a thud.

There were Vuitton suitcases all over the room. Enough for an entire *family*. In fact, some of them were so big you could put a family *in* them—the kids, at least.

"Close the door, why don't you?" said a bored British voice with a barely noticeable roll on the *r*. A girl stepped out from behind the wardrobe door.

Red hair in an explosion of curls.

Fishnet stockings to *here* and glossy Louboutin ankle boots.

Blue eyes that grabbed you and made you wonder why she was so . . . not interested in whether you took another breath.

Ever.

"Who are you?" How come no one had told me I was getting a roommate? And who could have prepared me for this, anyway?

"Mac," she said, returning to the depths of the wardrobe. Most people would have said, "What's your name?" back. She didn't.

"I'm Carly." Did I feel lame or what?

She looked around the door. "Pleasure. Looks like we're to be roommates." Then she went back to hanging things up.

There was no point in restating the obvious. I gathered my scattered brains and tried to remember what a good hostess was supposed to do. "Did someone show you where the dining room is? Supper is between five and six-thirty and I usually—"

"Carrie. I expected my own room," she said, as if I hadn't been talking. "Who do I speak to?"

"It's *Carly*. And Ms. Tobin's the dorm mistress for this floor."

"Fine. What were you saying about tea?"

I took a breath and remembered that one of us was what my brother calls *couth*. As opposed to *un*. "You're welcome to come with me and my friends if you want."

Pop! went the latches on one of the trunks. She threw up the lid and looked at me over the top of it, her reddish eyebrows lifting in amusement.

"Thanks so much. But I'll pass."

Okay, even I have my limits. I picked up my duffel, dropped it on the end of my bed, and left her to it. Maybe by the time I got back from tea—er, supper—she'd have convinced Ms. Tobin to give her a room in another dorm.

The way things looked, this *chica* would probably demand the headmistress's suite.

"What a *mo guai nuer*," Gillian said over her tortellini and asparagus. "I can't believe she snubbed you like that."

"You of all people," Lissa said, "who wouldn't hurt someone's feelings for anything."

"I wanted to," I confessed. "If I could have come up with something scathing. But you know how you freeze when you realize you've just been cut off at the knees?"

"What happened to your knees?" Jeremy Clay put his plate of linguine down and slid in next to Gillian. They traded a smile that made me feel sort of hollow inside—not the way I'd felt after Mac's little setdown, but still . . . like I was missing out on something. Like they had a secret and weren't telling.

You know what? Feeling sorry for yourself is not the way to start off a term. I smiled at Jeremy. "Nothing. How was your break? Did you get out to New York?"

He glanced at Gillian. "Yeah, I did."

Argh. Men. Never ask them a yes/no question. "And? Did you guys have fun? Shani said she had a blast after the initial shock."

Gillian grinned at me. "That's a nice way of saying my grand-mother scared the stilettos off her. At first. But then Nai-Nai realized Shani could eat even my brothers under the table no matter what she put in front of her, so after that they were best friends."

"My grandmother's like that, too," I said, nodding in sympathy. "She thinks I'm too thin so she's always making pots of mole and stuff. Little does she know."

It's a fact that I have way too much junk in my trunk. Part of the reason I'm majoring in history with a minor in fashion design is that when I make my own clothes, I can drape and cut to accentuate the positive and make people forget that big old negative following me around.

"You aren't too thin or too fat." Lissa is a perfect six. She's also the most loyal friend in the world. "You're just right. If I had your curves, I'd be a happy woman."

Time to change the subject. The last thing I wanted to do was talk about my body in front of a guy, even if he belonged to someone else. "So, did you guys get to see *Pride and Prejudice—The Musical*? Shani said you were bribing someone to get tickets."

"Close," Gillian said. "My mom is on the orchestra's board so we got seats in the first circle. You'd have loved it. Costume heaven."

"I would have." I sighed. "Why did I have to go to Veracruz for spring break? How come I couldn't have gone to New York, too?"

I hoped I sounded rhetorical. The truth was, there wasn't any money for trips to New York to see the hottest musical on Broadway with my friends. Or for the clothes to wear once I got there—unless I made them myself.

"That's it, then." Gillian waved a grape tomato on the end of her fork. "Next break you and Lissa are coming to see me. Not in the summer—no one in their right mind stays in the city in July. But at Christmas."

"Maybe we'll go to Veracruz," Lissa suggested. "Or you guys can come to Santa Barbara and I'll teach you to surf."

"That sounds perfect," I said. Either of Lissa's options wouldn't cost very much. New York, on the other hand, would. "I like warm places for my winter holidays."

"Good point," Gillian conceded. "So do I."

"Notice how getting through the last term of junior year isn't even on your radar?" Jeremy asked no one in particular. "It's all about vacations with you guys."

"Vacations are our reward," Gillian informed him. "You have to have something to get you through finals."

"Right, like you have to worry," he scoffed.

"She does," Lissa said. "She has to get *me* through finals."

While everyone laughed, I got up and walked over to the dessert bar. *Crème brulée*, berry parfaits, and German chocolate cake. You know you're depressed when even Dining Services' *crème brulée*—which puts a dreamy look in the eyes of just about everyone who goes here—doesn't get you excited.

I had to snap out of it. Thinking about all the things I didn't have and all the things I couldn't do would get me precisely nowhere. I had to focus on the good things.

My friends.

How lucky I was to have won the scholarship that got me into Spencer.

And how much luckier I was that in two terms, no one had figured out I was a scholarship kid.

Come on, Carly. Just because you can't flit off to New York to catch a show or order up the latest designs from Fashion Week doesn't mean your life is trash. Get ahold of your sense of proportion.

I took a berry parfait—blueberries have lots of antioxidants— and turned back to the table just as the dining room doors opened. They seemed to pause in their arc, giving my new roommate plenty of time to stroll through before they swung shut behind her. She'd changed out of the fishnets into a simple leaf-green dress with a black sweater and heels that absolutely screamed Paris—Rue de la Paix, to be exact. Number 11, to be even more exact. Chanel Couture.

My knees nearly buckled with envy.

"Is *that* your roommate?" Lissa asked.

Mac seemed completely unaware that everyone in the dining room was watching her as she floated across the floor like a runway model, collected a plate of Portobello mushroom ravioli and salad, and sat at the empty table next to the big window that faced out onto the quad.

Lissa was still gazing at her, puzzled. "I know I've seen her before."

I hardly heard her.

Because not only had the redhead cut into line ahead of Vanessa

Talbot, Dani Lavigne, and Emily Overton, she'd also invaded their prime real estate. No one sat at that table unless they'd sacrificed a freshman at midnight or whatever it was that people had to do to be friends with them.

When Vanessa turned with her plate, I swear I could hear the collective intake of breath as her gaze locked on the stunning interloper sitting with her back to the window, calmly cutting her ravioli with the edge of her fork.

"Uh oh," Gillian murmured. "Let the games begin."